The reviews a̲ ___ 　 　 ⅃ ⅃ ⅃
Lesbian Housewife

Some people think funny; some people write funny; Lorraine Howell lives funny. And, fortunately for us, she's elected to share her reality-is-stranger-than-fiction life with us in *"Memoirs of the Happy Lesbian Housewife – You Can't Make this Stuff Up, Seriously!"* A late blooming lesbian with three adult children, Howell has ample material from which to draw as she shares her tales of leaving her marriage, coming out and living happily ever after with her Sapphic love, Sweetie. Toss in Howell's southern-born-and-bred penchant for no-holds-barred storytelling and her "speak first, think later" approach to life and "Memoirs of the Happy Lesbian Housewife" is guaranteed to entertain.

Candy Parker, Contributing Editor, Lesbian.com

As modern as it is timeless, Lorraine *"The Happy Lesbian Housewife"* Howell's book, *"Memoirs of a The Happy Lesbian Housewife - You Can't Make This Stuff Up. Seriously!"* takes the reader on spirited rides through the amusement park of life. Often sweet, sometimes sardonic but never cynical, Ms. Howell paints vivid pictures of her unique but relatable tales with a poignant humor that will delight readers page after page.

Ellen Moschetto, Comedian, is a Boston-based Comedy Writer, Yoga Instructor, Podcaster on Project Fandom, Regular Daytime Job Holder and All-Around Nice Lady (usually). Follow Ellen on Twitter @EllenMoschetto

"Such a heart-felt, well-written book with plenty of chuckle out loud moments in The Happy Housewife's account of lesbian life. A totally great read and a much needed lesbian laugh-fest in our seemingly "serious world."

Denise Warner, www.MyLesbianRadio.com , Associate Editor / SHE Magazine/ www.shemag.com, Contributor: www.advocate. com

More reviews for - The Memoirs of a Happy Lesbian Housewife

The Happy Lesbian Housewife is laugh out loud hilarious! I want to shout it from the rooftops - The lesbian community has their very own Erma Bombeck! Lorraine Howell is the funniest author I've ever run across. I do want to add a warning - make sure you aren't drinking anything while reading this book. Seriously!

Yvonne Heidt, Multiple award winning author of Sometime Yesterday, The Awakening, Book One of the Sisters of Spirits Trilogy, and The Quickening Book Two in the SOS Trilogy.

"This book should come with a Warning Label: Don't read next to your sleeping partner or pets because you will scare the bejesus out of them when you bust out laughing!"

Liz McMullen, Author of If I Die Before I Wake and Hard Rock Candy and Talk Show host, www.thelizmcmullenshow.com

THE MEMOIRS OF THE HAPPY LESBIAN HOUSEWIFE

THE MEMOIRS OF THE HAPPY LESBIAN HOUSEWIFE

LORRAINE HOWELL

SAPPHIRE BOOKS

SALINAS, CALIFORNIA

ISBN - 978-1-939062-69-7

Editor - Heather Flournoy
Book Designer - LJ Reynolds
Cover - Leigh Hubbard

Sapphire Books
Salinas, CA 93912
www.sapphirebooks.com

Printed in the United States of America
First Edition – October 2014

This and other Sapphire Books titles can be found at
www.sapphirebooks.com

Acknowledgements

Sapphire Books, Chris, and Schileen: *Special thanks to you for not only taking a chance on a new author but a new(ish) genre in lesbian publishing: humor. I am so happy that you got my vision of wanting to make people laugh and supported it. I am at home with my Sapphire sisters and love you all. Thank you.*

Yvonne Heidt: *My "sister from another mister." I thank you for kicking my ass out of the nest…literally! This book would not have come to fruition without you. Thank you for always believing. I love you.*

Heather Flournoy: *To my wonderful editor I say thank you, thank you, thank you. You allowed me to keep my voice even when you did not quite understand it. I know that my "southern-isms" had to be difficult but you hung right in there with me. You have taught me so much and I appreciate you.*

Candy Parker: *You spotted me on a blog a few years ago and asked me to write for an online magazine. That is where "The Happy Lesbian Housewife" grew legs and took off. When we finally meet, I owe you a drink, my friend.*

Leigh Hubbard: *Thank you so much for coming up with the concept of what "The Happy Lesbian Housewife" looked like by looking at a picture of me and then reading my stories. You didn't take her too seriously and she is now a perfectly imperfect book cover.*

Liz McMullen and all of the Facebook Blitzing Ladies: *Liz, thank you for pulling me into your daily writing blitzes on Facebook. You and the other ladies that blitzed with us kept me honest and allowed me to finish my manuscript ahead of schedule. Here is a big ol' group hug for you all. Liz, I also thank you for reading my manuscript and giving me feedback. It really helped.*

Nicki Wachner: *Thank you for being you. You checked in with me every single day RE: my health, my progress in the book, or just to say "hi". That meant more to me than you can possibly know. I am pleased to have you as a new friend*

Carla Banks: *I don't even know where to begin... We have been best friends since we were 5 years old. I consider you my sister and I know that you feel the same. I also know that you have my back no matter what, and I have yours. Thank you for always being there and for always loving and supporting me. You accepted me & Sweetie when others did not. I love you from the very bottom of my heart and will always be here for you. By the way, you still owe me a new pair of shoes.*

Dedication

This, my first book, is dedicated to my family. Without them I would be nothing.

Bubba, the bravery that you have shown in the last few years and the choices that you have made even though they were not the easy ones, have made my heart swell with pride. I want to thank you for giving pa-pa permission to "go on to the other side." You did it with dignity and grace so that he could pass with the same dignity and grace. I thank you for that because I am not sure that I could have done it. I am also happy that you are now living your life your way. You are a wonderful son and father, and you deserve happiness. You have a whole new life to live. Be happy. You deserve it. I love you son.

Sissy, you have been through so much in your short life. Two brain surgeries and multiple illnesses have not stopped you or even slowed you down. As you work on your MSW while raising your son, I watch you with awe knowing that all you want to do is fix everyone and be the best wife, momma and daughter possible. You are 5'1" of courage and determination. Change the world Sissy. You can do it. I believe and I love you.

Buddy, you have always marched to beat of your own drummer and I truly admire that in you. You have done more, been to more places, met more people, and experienced more in 24 years than most people ever do. Thank you for getting me to New York and for experiencing all that it had to offer. Keep marching Buddy. There is so much more for you to do. "I love you right up to the moon – and back."

Sweetie, if I had my life to live over again, I would find you sooner so I could love you longer. Thank you for accepting me and my big ol' loud southern family and for loving us all unconditionally. I know that it can't always be easy. We all love you right back. You and I made a promise to each other to "Love deeply and laugh out loud every day." That is a promise that I will hold you to. I love you baby...Always!

Finally, Daddy, I wish you could have held on until I finished this but the damn beast (GBM) tore you from us too soon. I hope I made you proud daddy. I did it!

Introduction
(Or Should I Call It An "*OUTroduction?*")

"Cut the ending. Revise the script. The man of her dreams is a girl."
~ *Julie Anne Peters, Keeping You a Secret*

The Urban Dictionary defines "coming out" as the term used by lesbians, gays, bisexuals and transgendered to describe their experience of self-discovery, self-acceptance, openness and honesty about their sexual orientation and their decision to share this with others when and how they choose. Well, I have not chosen to share this fact with everyone just yet. I have a son that is a Baptist Youth Minister. Go figure! That's an easy share, right?

Since I am a "late in lifer," I have never had to actually tell anyone my sexual orientation. This daunting task loomed over my head like the proverbial black cloud. I was raised in Small Town, Georgia. I was afraid that by saying that I was gay out loud, I would be judged immediately and fall directly into the fiery pits of Hell. It happens that way you know. Just ask any good ol' boy Pentecostal Preacher from the Deep South. He'll tell you straight up.

"You are WHAT? Oh, you are like that." And then he will drop his wrist in the universal southern sign for gay, shake his head while "tsking" his tongue and proclaim rather loudly, "You are going to HELL!" Then, much like the game "Know or Go" that Ellen

DeGeneres plays on her talk show, Preacher man would hit a button that had mysteriously appeared from the ground and the earth would open up and down I would go! Straight into the bowels of Hades. There would be gnashing of teeth and rats and fire and shit. Seriously, that is what I was told. MY. WHOLE. FREAKING. LIFE. What many are still told. I believed it too. And people wonder why it is so hard to come out, especially in the Deep South. Come on down here, folks. Then you will understand. No wonder I'm a tad warped... although the medications do seem to help a bit!

By the way, where do you think those people go when Ellen hits the button in her "Know or Go" game? I mean I know they come back eventually but what happens in the interim? Maybe she is trying to "scare them gay" (toaster ovens all around people!), or she puts spells on them to make them convince all of their friends into watching her show so that her ratings consistently beat everyone like Katie Couric, Dr. Phil or the rest of those talk show people. Or maybe, and I hope this one is the winner, she is trying to undo all the damage that the aforementioned Pentecostal preachers have done so she has hypnotists waiting under that big box to do quickie hypnosis reminding everyone that falls through that they are "great just the way they are!"

(Note to self: DO NOT go on *Ellen* because she will spot me as damaged quickly and pick me for "Know or Go" and make me fall through the floor and I am afraid of falling through ANYTHING because of my neurotic trust issues.) Now back to the regularly scheduled story...or as Sweetie would say: "Squirrel!" This is her cute way of saying that I got sidetracked by something, anything. It happens. A LOT!

Truly all I really wanted, by coming out, was for

people to understand that by finally deciding to live my life with the woman of my dreams was that we were just like everyone else, and if they would just peek into our daily lives they would see that we laugh, cry, fight, and love just as they do. We buy groceries, clean house, and mow the lawn. We have family and pets. We are simply normal people with normal lives. Well, one of us is normal. I'm sort of, if you squint your eyes, stand on one foot, turn around backward then bend over and look between your legs at me, normal especially if I stay on the aforementioned meds. And I get sidetracked obviously. I know, shocking, right? But I'm not boring. Oh, and I talk to dead people. Honestly. More about that later. Like I said, never, ever boring!

Since I had yet to "come out" to my children, I decided that it would be a good idea to practice on others. This seemed a less scary idea. I had an appointment to see my doctor and thought that would be the perfect place to dip my toe in to test the waters. "Coming out" could be no worse than the burning hell of the bladder infection that I was suffering. Hell was hell no matter how you looked at it!

The morning of the appointment was agony. The sky was bleak. No birds were singing. The sun was not shining. My shoulders hunched forward and my heart was heavy. I swear I could hear the refrain of "Taps" playing in my mind. I am a grown-ass woman and I felt like a nine-year-old walking to the principal's office for writing dirty words on the blackboard behind the substitute teacher's desk. Really, really bad words that begin with "F" and "B." I can't say them here because I am only nine remember? Sheesh.

On arrival, I walked haltingly up the red brick stairs dragging one foot in front of the other. I reached the door and took a deep breath. The doorknob was only an inch from my outstretched hand when suddenly a skinny guy carrying a skateboard jerked the door open from the other side. I jumped back in terror. I was sure he could tell the real reason for my visit which made me blurt out, "It really burns when I pee. That's why I am here. Why are you looking at me like that? This is a very private issue."

"Whatever, weirdo," the skater guy mumbled.

I entered the waiting area, signed in and looked around the room. The other patients were staring at me curiously. Had they heard the exchange between me and skater guy? I lifted my chin and stared back defiantly. I had decided to do this. I could do this. I would do this. Really, I would!

I plopped into a faded gold brocade chair, grabbed a copy of *Good Housekeeping* off the teak coffee table and peeked over the top of the magazine. Across the room there was a red-haired woman in a purple flowing skirt. She was smiling kindly at me. I popped quickly back behind my magazine.

Why was she smiling? Did she KNOW that I was here to come out? Was it written all over my face? Good God. Was everyone's gaydar bouncing all over the place? I am such a femme. How could they know?

Next, I snuck a look at the man sitting on the sofa to my right and noticed that he had turned his attention back to his *Bloomberg Businessweek.*" He was a tall, thin, very stiff, conservative fella in a dark gray suit and tie and a light gray shirt. Even his shoes and briefcase were gray. Would he pull out an also-gray Gideon's Bible and smite me? *Stop it,* I thought. *You are so being paranoid.*

I frowned in dismay as I began to wonder about

my decision to out myself to my medical practitioner. Would I receive the same level of care? Would she still like me? Why did that even matter? Who was I? Sally Field? I was not winning an Oscar for God's sake! I was just telling her that I was gay. She was very young and hip and open. I figured that this would make it easier. I decided to just go for it. The thing was how to bring it up. I stared at the ceiling agonizing over how to do this. Sweat started pouring from my forehead as each approach at disclosure ran through my mind.

"Hey, yo, Doc, I'm a lesbian."

Nope. Too in your face. And who talks like that anyway? Certainly not me!

"Yes, Jen, (I call her Jen because we are close like that), I feel the need to share with you the fact that I am a lesbian. I was born this way but tried to live as a straight woman for many years. It has shaped me into the person that I am today."

Nope, that sounds just like an episode of Dr. Phil.

The nurse walked out and called "Bloomberg Bible" guy back. Her cheery voice had me jumping with fear and I grabbed for the Valium bottle in my black fringed purse. Inhaling deeply, I told myself I did not need a Valium. I was a strong woman. Then the ruminations in my brain began again.

"So, did you know that I'm gay?"

That might work. It was simple. Direct. To the point.

But when should I drop it into the conversation? While she was checking my reflexes? During my breast exam....Oh God! MY BREAST EXAMS! The horror! How about my Pap test. Oh my! How embarrassing! She may think I was coming on to her. Strike that. Paranoia was creeping in.

The nurse called my name. I shot out of the chair as if I had been caught masturbating right there in the waiting area. Purple skirt beamed at me compassionately. Why couldn't she go first? Why me? My legs felt like jelly and my mind was racing. Maybe I should have taken that Valium after all.

After the nurse walked me to my room, she handed me a paper gown, took my vitals and asked a few questions. All I could do was mutter my answers much like Jack Nicholson in *One Flew Over The Cuckoo's Nest* all the while thinking...

"How do you feel about homosexuals? I am one you know. A flaming lesbo, that's me."

That wouldn't work. I'm not a flaming anything and I really didn't care how anyone "felt" about my orientation. Or did I? Was that the reason that "coming out" was so hard? Did I care too much about what others thought of me? That was definitely something to think about at a later date.

Once the nurse left, I changed into the paper gown then picked at the ragged corner of the faded blue pleather table I was sitting on. Thoughts were whizzing around in my brain to the point that I needed Dramamine for motion sickness. Why was I so flustered?

Mad giggles then erupted as I thought of another way to introduce the topic.

"Say Doc, did you know that I prefer 'tweeters' over 'peters?'"

Totally juvenile. Funny as hell, but juvenile.

I then considered trying to impress my doctor with my command of facts.

"The Williams Institute at the UCLA School of Law estimates that there are 8.8 million gay, lesbian and bisexual persons in the U.S. based on the 2005/2006 American Community Survey. Well, I am one of them." She is intelligent. She likes facts and figures.

Ding, Ding, Ding! This just may be the winner. Thank you Google.

The door swung open slowly. I gasped for air. Into the stark white room walked the short, blonde and perky Dr. Jen. My mouth went dry. My hands shook. My armpits were drenched. Boob sweat caused the lovely paper gown to cling in all the wrong places. Not to mention what was happening in the nether regions …I was a hot mess! If I was having this hard of a time telling my cute little physician, how would I ever tell my preacher-son? Or, my ex-husband for that matter.

"Hi Hun, how are you today?" Dr. Jen asked, clipboard in hand.

"Fine," I squeaked, feeling as if I was clinging to the ceiling by my fingernails, my bare ass hanging out of the backless gown.

"You seem stressed. Are you drinking too much caffeine again?"

"Yes, caffeine! I drink too much caffeine. Stress, yes stress too. Too much stress." I blathered. I'm sure trepidation showed on my face.

"For heaven's sake girl, just calm down," she implored. "Tell me what brought you here today?"

The words didn't want to come out. I finally managed to croak, "I think I have a urinary tract infection."

While peering smartly at me over at me over the top of her glasses, Jen proceeded to ask all of the pertinent questions regarding my condition then sent me out to get a urine sample. I was a nervous wreck through every step. First, I couldn't get the lid off the

•

cup. I swear it was as if Thor had tightened it down himself. Once I finally got the cap off, I was shaking so badly that I peed all over my hand, all around the top of the cup and down the side of the toilet. Everywhere but inside the damn cup! I crossed my legs tightly to keep from peeing anymore, took a deep calming breath, wiped the beaker off, said a little prayer and vowed that I could do this. I uncrossed my legs and breathed out very slowly and a steady flow went right in the cup. Whew! Mission accomplished. I screwed the lid on and popped that puppy in the little window then went back to my room. After gathering all the data, Jen told me that I did indeed have a U.T.I. She prescribed some medication and went over all of the instructions that I needed in order to make sure that the infection went away and did not return. I tried to pay attention to her every word but I was fixated on telling her that I was gay and the only sounds that I was hearing coming from her lips were akin to Charlie Brown's teacher saying "WAAA WAAA....WAAA WAAA WAAA ."

She noticed my faraway look and snapped her fingers right in face. "Listen up you!"

I popped to attention.

"Here's what you need to do in addition to finishing the entire course of antibiotics. Water helps flush your urinary tract, so make sure you drink at least eight glasses daily."

"Does Diet Pepsi figure into that count, Doc?" I asked glibly.

She simply rolled her big blue eyes and continued. "Don't hold it when you need to urinate. And don't forget you should always wipe from front to back."

Ewwwwwww

"Taking showers instead of baths helps prevent

bacteria from entering the urethra and causing infection," she continued.

"Awwww, you know that I am a bath girl. C'mon, you are already taking my Diet Pepsi," I whined.

"Doctor's orders," she urged. "And, finally, always wash your genital area after intercourse to help prevent transferring bacteria and sperm from the vaginal area which can create a breeding ground for a U.T.I."

My head snapped up and my eyes sprung out like a cartoon character. ZOINKS! Here was the perfect opportunity.

"There is no sperm," I yelped. "None, nada, zilch zip, not an iota. Not anywhere, not anyhow. Don't have to worry about that one." I was practically shouting now. "I am an honest to goodness, card-carrying lesbian." My breath came out with a loud but very calming "*whoosh*."

There I said it. I looked down quickly; the ground did not open up and drop me into the abyss. No preacher mysteriously appeared to judge me. The sky did not spit hell fire and damnation upon me. All that happened was that I felt a huge sense of relief that I had finally told someone that was not technically just a "friend."

Dr. Jen did not faint, judge, condemn, or even bat an eyelash. She just said, "Well, then, that's a good thing. Why didn't you tell me before? I have lots of friends that are gay."

Wow. If she had lots of gay friends, maybe my other friends did too. Maybe this was just an issue in my own head. I was all worried for nothing. I hopped off of the blue pleather table and hugged her tightly, boob sweat and all. She left the room shaking her head, no doubt thinking that maybe I needed to see a psychiatrist. Little did she know that I already did.

I then dressed quickly, grabbed my prescriptions and skipped up to the front desk to pay while whistling a little ditty. There was a new spring in my step as I walked from the office. Birds sang gaily in the bright sunny sky. My shoulders were back. My chest was out. My heart was light.

At last I was ready. I could finally tell my preacher-son, Bubba. I knew just how to do it now. I started to go through the conversation in my mind:

"So son, do you ever get urinary tract infections? I actually know how to prevent those." Little did I know...

Yes, I Am an Adult Entertainer

"Everyone has talent. What is rare is the courage to
follow the talent to the dark place where it leads."
~Erica Jong

The small town of Boynton Beach in the
great state of Florida says that I am an adult
entertainer! At least that's what they told me when I went
to obtain my business license. Sweet little ol' me. The
mother of three grown children. An adult entertainer.
What the hell? Who'd pay to see me naked? Of course
the benefit to the city, and the biggest drawback to me,
was the prohibitive cost of being said adult entertainer.
It is very expensive to entertain adults! How the hell do
strippers afford a business license? Or even hookers for
that matter? And, while I didn't exactly do these things,
my business was basically for adults hence the "Adult
Entertainment" classification. I also could not operate
within a certain distance of schools or churches. How
rude. So, I did what any other "adult entertainer" would
do and moved my business to my home in a neighboring
city. Done deal.

The following week, I had a party at a client's
home. This was quite normal. I do a lot of these parties.
Yes, it was for adults. Yes, I would be entertaining
them. Whatever…I walked in and was greeted with the
normal stares, oohs, aahs, and hugs that I usually get.
There was also a level of shyness and fear which is to

be expected in my line of work. I immediately began to "work the room," getting some air kisses, "feeling" each woman in attendance, and getting a read on what each individual would want from me. Once I was acclimated to the room, I went to the front and had all of the ladies sit down in front of me to wait their turn. I lowered the lights, lit some scented candles, and put on some mood music. I could sense the eagerness of the lovely ladies to be picked first. The excitement was palpable and the heat was rising as I looked each of them in the eyes.

Suddenly, I felt a pull to my right and I saw an attractive brown-haired, blue-eyed female with the cutest dimples that I had ever seen. I suddenly knew that this was the woman of my dreams. GULP! I certainly did not need this. I was not looking for a woman of my dreams or any other kind of woman for that matter. Oh crap. Dimples was standing there with her hands in her pockets meeting my gaze hard. Hmmm, she was supposed to be sitting. She was a rule breaker. I love me a rule breaker. My heart was thumping loudly. My mouth was dry. This was not how I worked. I had to get myself together. I closed my eyes and breathed in deeply. I turned my head then reopened my own baby blues. I could not see Dimples from this vantage point. Whew, crisis averted! I could get to work...as long as I worked from the left side of the room.

The party continued at a good pace with me giving each client what she wanted or needed, whether it be in private or in front of the group. I did such a fabulous job that I brought several of the women to tears.

"Oh, my gosh. That was amazing!" from one red-haired client.

"How did you know what I needed?" from another.

"No one has ever been able to do that for me," said

a very professional, buttoned-up type.

"Ooooh, I am so glad that we found you," said a cute blonde. "I could stay all night!"

And on it went like that. However, each time that I came back around to Dimples, I could not perform. I felt like such a failure. This was my job. All these other women were sitting, jelly-like, with satisfaction on their faces and Dimples was still standing there, hands in pockets, scowling!

When it was finally it was time to go. I collected my payment, gave hugs and kisses all around, and shot out the door like a rabid dog was chasing me. I had let a client down. I had pleased thirteen women but disappointed THE ONE and it felt bad. I had wanted so badly to gratify Dimples. Damn it, I wanted another chance. What was this all about? I usually left a party and let it go. Moved on. Forgot about it. And all I wanted to do was see her again. Make things right. But that ship had sailed. I didn't even know her name. I had given everyone my card but why would she use it after the letdown that I had just served her. "DAMN. DAMN. DAMN," I cursed as a tear trickled down my cheek.

I was worn slap-out so I went home and slept for two straight days. It takes a lot out of a woman to give everything to thirteen ladies. Once I woke up, I thought of little but Dimples. This was so out of character for me that I thought I was quite possibly going bonkers. I was sitting by the phone every minute like a seventh grade girl waiting for that person she has her eye on to call, but it was never my dimpled-cheek crush. I just knew that if I could set up a personal appointment with Dimples, I could meet her wishes. *Ring, phone, ring.*

Suddenly it did! And it was our area code. I jumped straight out of my chair and peed myself just a little bit. (Don't judge! You've done it too!) "Please let this be her," I whispered.

"HELLO," I screeched. "Umm...I mean, hello, may I help you?" I intoned in my sexiest phone voice.

"Hello," articulated a very professional voice. "I was at the party last Friday..."

My hopes soared as I interrupted, "Yes, yes." I recognized the voice. It was HER! I began doing a happy dance around the dining table while holding my crotch to keep from peeing myself again. I really must do something about this bladder issue.

"As I was saying, I was at the party and I didn't get..." She began again sounding none too pleased to have been interrupted.

"Oh, I am so sorry! I know that I did not give you what you wanted but if you choose to come in for a personal appointment, I will do my very best this time. I surely will. When would you like to come to my HOME office to see me?" I was still stammering as I accentuated the word "home" a bit but what the hell? I was getting her to come in. Oh yes I was!

"How about next Monday?" she inquired.

"How about tomorrow?" I countered.

You have an appointment THAT soon?" She sounded a bit confused as I am usually booked weeks in advance. As I said, I am good at what I do!

"Oh yes," I lied straight through my teeth. I most certainly did NOT have an appointment that SOON. I was booked for three weeks but for Dimples I could —and would—be ready in two hours flat!

"I'll take it," she responded. "I will leave work early. Text me your address. I will not be late and I don't expect you to be either."

"Oh, no, I won't be. No worries there. I am never

late. Never, ever, nope," I fibbed as I was making my incessantly late self a sticky note to cancel each and every appointment for tomorrow.

ୠୠୠୠୠ

The next day came way too soon, yet not soon enough. 3:00 p.m. seemed an eternity away yet I knew that it would take me that long to prepare myself and my office. I primped and preened, put on my makeup, and tried on outfit after outfit. I tried on black as it is slimming, then blue to bring out my eyes. Next came green as a contrast to my blonde hair. I finally settled on a flowing rainbow colored top and jeans–the combo covered the entire color wheel. My poor dog was running around like a crazy mutt. She was picking up on my anxiety. Then it was time to do my hair. Hmmm… curly or straight? I went straight for this session. Feeling as if I looked my best, I left my bedroom, which now looked like it had been hit by the same tornado that had carried Dorothy to Oz. I headed downstairs, leaving the tornado in my wake. That mess most definitely could wait. I had business to attend to. Next, I began in my office. I dimmed the lights, lit the candles and incense, fluffed the pillows, adjusted the blanket, then sat down to wait. It was 8:30 a.m. I still had six and a half hours to go. That was okay…at least I would not be late! I could be patient. NOT! So, I did my hair and makeup again. That took me to 9:40 a.m. Screw it. I curled up with my doggy and took a nap.

At 12:45 p.m. I woke with a start. I had to eat lunch. I would need my strength. I needed to satisfy this woman of my dreams. I fixed a sandwich and grabbed a soda from the fridge, then sat down to gobble it all down and realized that I couldn't eat due to my nerves, so my sweet pooch got a special treat of ham and cheese. Then I went frantically back upstairs to redo my makeup and dress again, this time in pink to match the streak in my hair. When this was done, I came back downstairs and fluffed the pillows AGAIN and re-straightened the already straightened house. I lost track of time as I was thinking of Dimples and suddenly the doorbell rang. I jumped right out of my jewelry! Have you ever seen jewelry just hang in mid-air? It is way cool until it falls on your head and slaps you square in the face. Then it just hurts. (Note to self: Do not wear such heavy jewelry!) I grabbed the jewelry and shoved it under the sofa cushion and sauntered (read that as "Ran like a bat out of hell") to the front door. I said coolly, "Who is it?" As if I didn't already know.

"It's your three o'clock appointment," she answered dryly.

I rose up and looked out the peephole and there she stood: the woman of my dreams. I grabbed for the doorknob and suddenly my muscles just froze! I could not move my arm.

She rang the bell again. I whispered to my hand, "Open the door now. Just turn the freaking knob and OPEN. IT!" Nothing! My own arm was betraying me. Fear set in. Would she leave? Oh no. Please, no! I slid slowly down the wall.

She knocked. LOUDLY! "Hello, I know you are in there. You talked to me and I can still hear you breathing. Panting really. Are you okay? Open the door. Do you need an ambulance?"

The earsplitting knock scared the crap out of me and I jumped straight up and was finally able to maneuver the doorknob open by using both floppy, fishlike hands and my right foot. I stepped back and invited Dimples in, hair and clothing askew and suddenly my sweet, loving miniature pinscher promptly bit her right on the ass. What a great start! A crazy floppy armed lady that couldn't force a door open and a rabid biting dog.

"OH. MY. GOD. I am so sorry," I yelped as I grabbed the offending pup up and shoved her in a spare bedroom.

"No problem. She just got my pants. No skin involved...well, not much anyway. What's her name? Cujo?"

At the mention of skin, I blushed. What was it with this woman? Sheesh, I had to get a grip. "No, no, it's Juno. She doesn't always act like that...just sometimes...I don't know..." I prattled.

"Just joking. I'm fine. Are you okay though? Do you think we can do this?" She probed.

"Come on back," I said in my very best sultry squeak while smoothing my hair. I feared that I sounded like a boy hitting puberty but, by damn, I was trying!

We went into my dim, candlelit, sweet-smelling office and sat down across from each other. This was the "get to know each other phase," since I had failed so miserably at that the last time. I reached out to touch her hand and sparks flew. NO, I mean literal sparks! Blue ones. I saw them. Really, I did! We began to chat. This was the prelude to my being able to give her what she wanted. I looked deeply into her beautiful baby blue eyes while clutching her hand. I did all the things that I usually do. I concentrated. I felt. I touched. I. GOT. NOTHING!

"Well...uh...I...umm...feel like I should sit closer to you so that I...umm...can...," I yammered.

"Nothing, huh?" She said succinctly. She was

smart, this one.

"NO! What is wrong with me? I want to give you what you need but I just can't figure out how to do it or even what IT is. Pleasing you is so very important to me and I got nothin'!" I was devastated.

"That's okay. At least you didn't lie and act like you knew what I wanted or worse, try and force something on me. I respect that," She said as she stood to leave.

She respected me! Wow. Cool. I was dancing on the inside while trying to look all nonchalant on the outside.

"Are you okay?" She asked. "Your face is sort of scrunched up and your fists are drawn up into balls. You are also twitching a bit. Are you having a stroke? I knew something was wrong when I got here."

So much for nonchalance. "Nope, I'm good. Job hazard," I squeaked like a mouse. I was walking her to her truck by this time. I must have looked like Quasimodo dragging along beside her. How sexy is that visual? I know right? How could she resist me?

"If you say so. Now, how much do I owe you?" She queried as she got into her vehicle.

I replied, "Nothing. I gave you nothing so you owe me nothing."

Her retort was, "I can't do that. I took up your time so I owe you something. I insist!"

"How about a drink?" I looked around. Surely I didn't just say that. It couldn't have been me. I didn't do things like that. But, as I perused the area, there was no one else there. What in the world was wrong with me?

"Only if that drink includes dinner," Dimples smirked.

"Absolutely," I shrilled.

"Tomorrow night. Seven o'clock. Be ready." She

took charge.

I cleared my throat and murmured, "I will," and I watched her drive away. My heart was soaring. What would I wear? I should get my nails done. My hair needed cutting. I ran back into the house to prepare.

≈ ≈ ≈ ≈

Dimples picked me up precisely at 7:00 PM the following night (What did you expect for heaven's sake?), and we headed out for our first date...squeal! I must say that it was wonderful! We drove slowly; chatting along the way (okay, I chatted, she listened), had Mexican food, and talked about my kids and her job and various other weird subjects that popped into my mind. I did decide beforehand that my job was off the table for discussion that night. Especially after two such epic failures! When we finished our dinner AND drinks (more drinks for me than for her...Hey, I was a nervous wreck!), we went back to her place and watched a movie. I don't remember what it was. I was too busy concentrating on her holding my hand (Everybody now...Awwwwww) to even pay attention to what was on the television. I was also trying to figure out if I stuck my finger in her dimple to see exactly how deep it was if she'd think I was too weird. I decided she would. So I did it anyway. It's pretty deep. Even though she must have thought was I was a wee bit crazy, it didn't stop us from making out a bit during the movie. OH. MY. SWEET. JESUS. Was this what it was supposed to be like? Why, yes, I do believe it was! She was, after all, the woman of my dreams.

That, my friends is how Sweetie and I came to be.

⚗⚗⚗⚗

Addendum

Alright you dirty minded people, get your minds out of the gutter. I am, for the purpose of business licenses (in some counties), an "Adult Entertainer." This does not mean that I dance on poles or give any other sexual favors, though I do not judge those that do. I do give pleasure, although not in the way you little pervs might have been thinking. I am a professional psychic medium. I give pleasure by connecting the living to those that have crossed over or by giving answers to pressing questions. I am very good at what I do. I just can't read those that are too close or going to become too close to me such as family or partners. Hence, the reason I couldn't read Sweetie. I have been on TV and everything. Put your search engine down, you won't find me under this name. Intrigued? Want to know my real name? I can be bought. Just send a nice piece of jewelry (I really like turquoise) in care of my publisher and I will send you my name. (My publisher won't let me take cash. Everybody now... BOOOO!) HA, HA! Just kidding! I'll take gift cards. No, really just research me or send Diet Pepsi. OK. No gifts... Sheesh, google me or something. I'm not that hard to find.

Happy reading!

Be very, very quiet
A Totally True Text Message

Bubba: Mom, I got a note from Riley's teacher today.

Me: Another one?

Bubba: Yes, but this one concerned you.

Me: Me? What'd I do?

Bubba: Well according to the note, it's not good!

Me: We are a country away. How can I get in trouble that far from you?

Bubba: It's your job!

Me: My job is to get in trouble?

Bubba: No goofy, your work job!

Me: Huh?

Bubba: Yup! Evidently today was some sort of job fair where they discussed different types of jobs and they found your job to be a little, shall we say, immoral?

Me: Immoral? WTF?

Bubba: Well, you know when we came to visit and you had to work that one day?

Me: Yeaaaa....

Bubba: And you sent the girls downstairs and told them to be quiet for a little while...

Me: Oh sheesh, what did she tell them?

Bubba: Well, she did not lie. She simply told her teacher what you said...verbatim! She told her that her Mimi "worked in her pajamas, in the bedroom with the door locked and that she and Rosie had to stay downstairs and be very, very quiet so that Mimi's clients wouldn't hear them. That Mimi would only be up there for about two hours in order to "take care" of two clients but, after that, Mimi would be free to play all the rest of the day!" ROFL...do you know what that sounds like mom?

Me: OMG! Of course I do. I sound like a hooker or a phone sex operator! Did you at least call her teacher and explain that I am a psychic medium and do phone conferences?

Bubba: Nope, not yet. I think I will just let this one simmer over the weekend.

Me: BUBBA!!!

Bubba: Love you mom!

Me: Call that teacher now. I mean it Bubba!

Bubba: :)

We Are Lesbian, Hear Us Roar

"I am a rare species, not a stereotype."
~ Ivan E. Coyote

"What does a lesbian bring on a second date? A U-Haul." Ummm...ok so we didn't do it quite that quickly, but we did it. After months of dating, we moved in together! We have a life. We have love. We have a family. Sweetie "inherited" my two sons and my daughter as well as my three granddaughters and a grandchild on the way. We also have a neurotic little dog, a very large goofy dog, and a weird cat. So there, we are officially a couple. My big question now is: **"Where is my toaster oven dammit?"**

If you don't understand what I mean by that, well, crawl out of your hole and let me explain it to you. Some really prominent lesbian, who a big giant search engine could not narrow down for me, made the toaster oven joke famous. The joke is based on the premise that there is some secret-society lesbian recruiting service – kind of like Amway – that gives out toaster ovens when you "turn someone gay." So Sweetie, who in some people's eyes converted little ol' me, told me that we would get a toaster oven. Well, how exciting! I have always wanted a toaster oven. We have been living together for months now and our new toaster oven has still not arrived. I do the biggest part of the cooking and could really use this gift in the kitchen.

Does anyone know how long the oven takes to arrive after the "conversion?" Is there a time specification to see if the lesbianism "sticks" after said conversion? Who can I ask? Who is in charge of the secret-society lesbian recruiting service? If anyone out there has the phone number, could you please send it to me in care of my publisher? It would be much appreciated as I am on a budget and getting the aforementioned FREE toaster oven would make me such a happy camper...well, we don't really camp like most lesbians do because Sweetie is afraid of creepy-crawlies, but you know what I mean. I would appreciate any answers, phone numbers, or secret society addresses that anyone may have. I will let you all know when the oven arrives. Hell, I will even invite you over for Baked Ziti! That way we can partake in another of the truly fun lesbian events – The Potluck Dinner!

The potluck dinner works thusly: a group of lesbians actually put on their bras, grab a clean pair of cargo shorts and a gray T-shirt, jump in their various trucks or SUVs, and drive to a sister-lesbian's house for fun, food and fellowship...or should that be galship? It is an extra added bonus if there is some type of sporting event on. My favorite is football. Go Broncos! (Shameless plug here as Sweetie loves the Cowboys. We are a house divided on this matter). All of the nice lesbian sisters bring their best dish with a side of granola and everyone just pigs out. Or, in our case, our friend Diddy makes everything much like a gourmet chef would and the rest of us just show up with half of an old pound cake, leftover spinach dip that has turned gray or moldy cheese, or a single apple. We do this because we know that no one is going to eat what we bring because Chef Diddy is on duty. We gather around her sumptuous spread and ooh and aah a bit then dig in as we start to discuss how many babies, dogs and/or cats we have or are going to adopt. Next on our agenda is NEW TATTOOS! How exciting. We all tend to get new ones every month or so and showing them off is imperative. We make it into a contest as dykes are über competitive. This time it is a tight race between Chris's dancing hula girl and Mel's "I Hate Men" lettering with a fist coming down to squash the word "Men." After much debate, Mel takes it. The line work in the fist is just too good and everyone knows that all lesbians hate men except, of course, for our own children, brothers, fathers and gay male friends. Speaking of men, they are not allowed at our little soirées unless they happen to be our children. Joe is always there. He is our nephew and is such a handsome young lad. Bless his poor heart, always surrounded by so much estrogen. I gotta say though, he always hangs right in there. When we start gabbing, he yanks out the Xbox controller and puts on his headphones. Smart kid, that boy. Since Joe has his headphones on, now is the time to talk about the size, texture and shape of our new strap-on. The femmes get together and twitter over color and sparkles in their "toys" while the butches worry more about size and ease of use in their "gear."

While we are talking, I look around the room with camaraderie and love. These are my people and I am pleased to notice that we are all holding true to form. All of the coupled ladies have a butch and a femme. We do this because it is so much easier for straight folks to figure out which of us is the male and which is the female in the relationship. We are always trying to make things easier for the straight world. We are good like that. Heck, femme on femme or butch on butch can be so confusing, even to us card-carrying lesbians.

This brings up another point. "The Lesbian Card." Every good lesbian has one. You don't? Well, you better check yourself, missy! I haven't been "out" long enough to get my toaster oven, but I have my card. This is of utmost importance. What if you get carded at a pride event or a gay bar? You, my dear, are busted! You got nothing! So get your Lesbian Card... what are you waiting for? NOW! Wait, I think you need a recommendation or something. Ask your partner or lover or an older dyke for the information. They should know exactly what to do. My wife took care of it for me. She tends to threaten on a daily basis that I am "about to lose my card" for some silly infraction like not knowing which screwdriver is a Phillips head or flat head, so study up on "dykey" things before you get yours or they just might yank it away as quickly as you got it. Just sayin'.

When you receive your Lesbian Card, you will also receive "The Book." This book lists all of the lesbians in the whole, wide world. It is kind of like a witch's book of spells. When a lesbian is "converted," her name automatically appears in every single book in the realm along with a very flattering picture. It is magic really. This way when your sister in Alaska asks you, who lives in Florida, "Oh my neighbors' daughter's college roommate, Cindy, is gay. Do you know her?" You can simply look her up in "The Book" and assure your sister that indeed you do know Cindy! Very helpful, this little book.

One other thing that I have learned is that it is always imperative to help a "sistah" out! This means that if you go into a store, need a plumber, want a new car or are in the market for a new house, you should always look for a sister-lesbian that is a professional in that area. It really doesn't matter if they are competent or not as long as they are "sistahs." All that really matters is that you are keeping *our* money working for *our* team!

C'mon all my sister-lesbians and raise your feminist fists in solidarity with me! The solidarity to rid the world of these and other stereotypes that follow us daily. Let us be known as what we are: Women, lovers, couples, families, and people. Just like everyone else. That is all.

♫ ♫ ♪ ♪

Addendum

This was written totally tongue-in-cheek except for the part about solidarity, ridding the world of stupid stereotypes, and Chef Diddy. She is an amazing cook that never ceases to amaze at our potlucks...Okay, the potluck part is true too...but just because we all really like each other. Anyway, maybe I'll get some of Chef Diddy's desserts or mushrooms on the grill or potato salad out of this. Why'd you think I mentioned her cooking? Geeze, I'm no dummy! Just joking, Diddy. You know we all love you...And your cooking...So, hook a sistah up.

The Day I Almost Killed Sweetie
Or
OCD Is More Serious Than I Thought

"I'm not really OCD but...can I show you the RIGHT
way to do that?"
~Unknown

If you are offended by the idea of looking at the humorous side of OCD, you may not want to continue reading this little story. This is because I find the fact that Sweetie suffers from a mild form of this disorder absolutely hilarious. She, however, swears vehemently that she does not have even the tiniest bit of the malady. I did my research. Web MD is a wonderful thing. Sweetie's symptoms popped up on my computer screen like Punxsutawney Phil on Groundhog Day!
   *Fear of dirt or contamination by germs.
   *Need for order, symmetry, or exactness.
   *Refusing to shake hands or touch doorknobs.
   *Constantly arranging things in a certain way.
   I could go on and on...
   Sweetie says that she is just neat and likes everything, such as canned corn, to have a place and for everything to be in that place at all times. I, on the other hand, could care less where the canned goods go as long as they are in the general vicinity of the cabinet. Sweetie also says that germs are not our friends and

should be avoided at all costs. I, however, subscribe to the five second rule. As long as the food that you drop on the ground outside of Sonic Drive-In only stays there five seconds or less...it is still good! When I grab a French fry off the food stained concrete and pop it in my mouth, Sweetie starts to tic. Her head twitches to the side and her face scrunches up a bit like Popeye. I hear a whoosh escape her mouth followed by a gagging noise. For shits and giggles, I will usually drop another fry and count to four then grab it and shove it in my mouth. This could go on for an entire meal. Talk about dining entertainment!

When Sweetie and I first got together, I had to be "trained." No joke. Like a dog. Taught, instructed, tutored. I halfway expected my nose to be rubbed in pee and my ass to be slapped with a newspaper when I got things wrong. My training started early one Saturday morning and my first lesson concerned toilet paper. How hard could that be? Little did I know...

I have always been a good student, an overachiever really, so I followed Sweetie around and took notes. I was determined to be a dutiful wife. She started by saying that toilet paper must ALWAYS roll over the top. It is more efficient that way. Over also reduces the risk of accidentally brushing the wall or cabinet with one's knuckles which could transfer grime and germs to said person's tweeter area. Ewww...who thought of that? Now I had a visual that I may have a hard time getting rid of. I began to wonder if one could bleach one's eyes to get rid of icky images.

Next, I had to learn that the tags on all bed covers SHOULD be at the bottom of the bed. Okay, I can agree with that one. Also, pillow cases MUST always have the opening facing toward the outside of the bed.

This has something to do with germs spewing out toward our faces while we sleep. That's what you want to think about before dozing off to a night of blissful repose huh? There is also an aesthetic value to this rule but mostly it's all about spewing germs. I had never even thought of that before but thanks for the graphic Sweetie!

The next lecture was that all canned goods should be separated by type and should all face forward in exactly the same manner. Corn goes with corn, green beans with green beans, tomato soup with tomato soup, etc. Moving forward with this, pasta is separated by type, cereal by kind, and even Pop-Tarts have their own special place. Holy shit! How long did it take this woman to put up groceries? I won't even get into the cleaning supplies.

There were also directives on how to buy lottery tickets. It is always three Powerball tickets and two Lotto tickets. They must be bought by Sweetie at the same Mobile station on Wednesday only. She has never won jack shit so I question her rules a bit...but whatever.

I glanced down at my notes:

*Corn goes on the lower far right of the cabinet

*Spaghetti sauce goes in the upper left corner

*Toilet paper, Angel Soft only, must roll over the top for efficiency

*The guest room lamp must be turned on at 6:45 p.m.

*BLAH, BLAH

*BLAH

*B....

I started to zone out when suddenly a plot began to hatch in the very dark recesses of my mind. I continued to follow Sweetie around. She thought I was being such an attentive partner. I was really making notes on how to drive her bat-shit crazy.

About a week later, I put my plan into action. While Sweetie was at work on a Tuesday, I got busy. I thought that I would start by being a good "little woman" and went to the Hess station to buy one Lotto and four Powerball tickets. I then drove to the grocery store and made purchases needed to put my ideas into play. I skipped gaily back to the car and headed home. Into the house and off to work I went.

Nothing was left untouched. I started in the master bathroom where I put a roll of Charmin on the spool. It was rolling from the underneath and I let it fall into a pool on the floor. Next I went into the bedroom where I placed the sheets with the tag at the top of the bed. The pillowcases all were placed so that the opening was facing inward. Germs be damned!

Next came the kitchen. I mixed all of the vegetables together. Corn and green beans were stacked together. I placed spaghetti sauce with the cereal. Everything was facing a different way. It was all willy-nilly! The sodas in the refrigerator went where the milk should be and I put the cheese in with the fruit. I grabbed the potato chips and placed them on the dining room table along with my nail polish and a cheese grater for good measure.

Giggles started to rumble through me as I went into the guest room and turned on the lamp at 4:15. I then went into the guest bathroom and took that roll of toilet paper off of the spool and placed it on the sink. Gales of laughter burst from my throat. I was behaving like a mad woman. Suddenly I heard Sweetie's truck in the driveway. I ran into the living room and plopped down on the sofa, grabbed a magazine and pretended to read as if nothing was amiss.

Sweetie walked in the door and immediately knew something was awry. She tilted her head back and forth like a puppy watching a tennis match. She sniffed the air. She looked around. A yelp escaped her lips. She felt it. Something was different. Up the stairs she ran into the bedroom. Silence. The bathroom was next. More silence. I began to feel fearful. Sweetie ran back to the living room and noticed that the guest room light was already on and it was only 5:15 PM. Also, there was "stuff" on the dining table. Sweetie hates "stuff" being anywhere. Her hands began to shake as she made the turn into the kitchen. A loud scream emanated from her very core. I heard the cabinets open and then a loud thud. I jumped straight up from my seated position and ran in panic to see what was going on. Sweetie was in a heap on the floor. Her eyes were closed and drool was trickling from the corner of her mouth. I had taken it too far. Her heart couldn't take all this at one time. I had killed her.

I squatted down beside her to see if I should do CPR. She opened her eyes a little bit and moaned. She was still alive. Whew, I felt relief. I wouldn't do well in jail. I patted her hand and assured her that she would be okay…I hoped. She looked up at me as if struggling to get out words. I leaned closer in order to hear her. What if these were her last words. Holy shit!

"Please tell me that you used the lint roller on the sheets before you made the bed and that you didn't use my deodorant again. You know I hate fuzzies and sharing deodorant is gross…ack the germs!" She was finally able to force out. Seriously? That was what she had to say? Those could possibly be her final words to me. She had scared the hell out of me. Then I noticed it: a green M&M on the floor. An evil grin split my

face while Sweeties eyes followed my hand as I slowly
picked up the green circle of sweetness and popped it in
my mouth. Sweetie's eyes rolled back again. Evidently
OCD is a little more serious than I realized. I laid her
head gently on the kitchen floor and sniggering, went
back to my weekly issue of my favorite gossip magazine.

A Day in the Life of the Happy Lesbian Housewife
A (Mostly) True Story

"I don't pretend to be an ordinary housewife."
~Elizabeth Taylor

Recently I have received a couple of emails and comments regarding the whole "Happy Lesbian Housewife" thing. Most are supportive but one, in particular, was a bit judgmental. The woman that wrote this particular email asked me to explain exactly what a "lesbian housewife" is and then went on a diatribe about how I was setting feminism back by a hundred years! Wow, I did not realize that I had that much power...little ol' me? I can set feminism back a hundred years just by writing about my little ol' life? COOL!

I decided to address the issues that she had by allowing everyone to have a peek inside my daily life as a wonderfully fulfilled, superbly happy, partner-pleasing, lesbian housewife. Even though Sweetie and I are not "married", this is what I consider myself to be. Sit back, hold on and enjoy the ride!

5:00 AM ~ I spring from the bed with joy in my heart and full, if somewhat smeared, makeup on and I'm ready to start my day. I pull on my flannel apron, but nothing else cuz that's how Sweetie likes me (wink,

wink), then rush downstairs to let the dogs out and begin a load of laundry before preparing breakfast for my love. I have trained the dogs to go outside quietly so as not to awaken Momma with their frisky gamboling.

6:00 AM ~ I go upstairs to gently awaken Sweetie with a heartfelt kiss upon her lovely, full lips. She hates to be woken abruptly so I am careful to bring her into her day gradually and tenderly. I tell her that her breakfast is almost ready but that she has time for a warm shower, which is already running for her. She looks at me lovingly as she slips out of bed and into her waiting robe, which has been warmed in the dryer. As she showers, I iron and lay out her clothing for the day.

6:45 AM ~ I put a homemade apple strudel on the table and call my honey down to breakfast. The dogs have been fluffed and look lovely as they greet their Momma with a sweet lick to the top of her hand. We eat a scrumptious meal while discussing our plans for the day.

7:15 AM ~ Sweetie goes out to sit on the patio for a smoke while I clean up the table and start a load of dishes in the dishwasher. I also use this time to feed the sweet doggies and clean up any mess they may have made.

8:00 AM ~ As Sweetie gets ready for work, I change the sheets and make the bed, then start another load of laundry. I also use this time to prepare lunch for my honey so that I know she eats healthy during the day. I drop in a little note to remind her of my love. I seal it with a kiss. Oh, how I adore this woman!

8:30 AM ~ I make sure that Sweetie has everything that she needs for her day and send her on her way with another long, lingering kiss. The dogs bid her goodbye by waving their sweet little tails just as I taught them to do.

9:00 AM ~ I clean, dust and vacuum the living room and bathrooms while listening to Melissa Etheridge on my iPod.

9:45 AM ~ I run a warm bath for myself. While it is running, I use my most expensive wrinkle creams so that I won't get all furrowed. I really want to continue to look good for my dearest for as long as possible. I get in the bath and soak for a while, shaving so that I do not have prickles. I wouldn't want to chafe my honey with hairy legs. I mean, seriously, how inconsiderate would that be?

10:15 AM ~ I get dressed, freshen my makeup and hair and then go downstairs to start a casserole for lunch. I let the dogs out to have a bit of free play time. While they are frolicking, I pick some veggies and slay a fowl for tonight's dinner. Sweetie likes her food fresh and it's the least that I can do for her health, right?

11:00 AM ~ I settle in front of the television with a cup of tea and some bon-bons and watch Ellen.

12:00 PM ~ I turn the television off, let the dogs in, and grab the casserole out of the oven. It is time to head out to a potluck luncheon at the country club with all the other happy lesbian housewives. We have a great time eating while we discuss Ellen, recipes, and the best way to wash flannel and shine Doc Martens in order to get the ultimate gloss for our honeys. We then speak about how to keep our lovers happy…you know, in the sack (wink, wink). Today, we also have a spirited discussion on whether or not the latest in a long line of young B-listers in Hollywood is really gay and whether or not, if we were single, we would "hit that." I would not! She is definitely not my type. I am not sure whose type she is as none of my potluckers jumped on it.

1:30 PM ~ I finally make it back to the Jeep and pop in my k.d. lang CD. I drive to the nail salon singing "She was a big boned gal from southern Alberta, you just can't call her small and you can bet every Saturday night, she'd be headed for the legion hall...YEEHAW!" Love me some k.d.! It's time for my mani/pedi. Today's polish is "Red Zen." Sweetie loves this color! She says it is sexy. Looking sexy leads to getting some sex and, seriously, ain't that what we housewives are after anyway? I know this one is!

2:30 PM ~ After my mani/pedi, I stop in at my favorite bookstore to check out the lesbian section for any new fiction. Linda Kay Sylva has a new book out. The Demon Hunter series is damn good! I check out all of Sapphire Publishing's new releases. They are really putting out some good stuff. I settled on *Last Train* by Isabella for tonight's reading pleasure... and I do mean **pleasure!** It is a little erotic gem that should get me laid if I recite it out loud with just the right inflection in my voice (read that: If I use my phone sex voice). I also check out the *Lesbian Kama Sutra* for any new and exciting sexual positions that my lover may like. Gotta keep things exciting you know! Today, I get lucky and find a great one. Somebody's going to be happy tonight if I can get my lower half to twist so that my left leg goes over my right shoulder. I think I can, I think I can!

3:30 PM ~ I stop in at the mall for a bit of shopping with Sweetie's credit card. She may earn the money, but I can spend it! I immediately find some cute lingerie. Oh, it is surely going to be a good night in the Howell house tonight. On the ride home I stop at Starbucks for a latté...skinny of course. I must keep my girlish figure for my baby. Once home, I let the dogs out and finish up any housework not completed earlier.

5:00 PM ~ I begin dinner preparations while starting an episode of "The L Word" from my boxed set. I just love that Shane! That girl is so hot! Dinner tonight is going to be baked chicken, which you may remember I killed myself earlier in the day. I will also be fixing new potatoes and green beans from my very own garden which were picked at the peak of perfection this very morning. As dinner is cooking I take a few moments to freshen up so that I look and smell my best when Sweetie gets home.

6:00 PM ~ Time to turn off the television and put on some sexy music for when my one and only walks in the door. Tonight's soundtrack includes: *"The Promise"* by Tracy Chapman, *"Alright"* by Kinnie Starr, and *"Make Yourself Comfortable"* by Sarah Vaughn. Can I pic some good music or what? I am setting the scene for later.

6:15 PM ~ I put on my sexy new lingerie and perfume and head downstairs while singing along with Tracy's "Baby Can I Hold You." "But you can say baby, Baby can I hold you tonight? Maybe if I told you the right words, at the right time you'd be mine." Such touching words. Sweetie would love to hear this relaxing yet sexy song as she came inside after her long, hard day.

6:18 PM ~ I line the dogs up at the door. They look so cute with their tails all brushed out. They wait excitedly, as do I, for the sound of the truck in the driveway.

6:20 PM ~ Momma's home! I greet her at the door with a nice cold beer with lime and a sweet kiss. The dogs walk passively over and kiss her hand ever so lovingly. We are joyful to have her home! The look on her face when she sees the new lingerie makes me melt.

6:30 PM ~ Sweetie's eyes glow with pride as I lay out the chicken and vegetables on the table before her. We eat while discussing her day, the dogs lying at our feet. What a perfect evening.

7:00 PM ~ As Sweetie heads to the patio for a smoke, I clean up the kitchen, feed the dogs, and turn down our bed. I then lay out her pajamas and spritz my perfume on the sheets so that it reminds her of me. She comes in and changes while I let the dogs out.

8:00 PM ~ My honey and I snuggle on the sofa while watching *Survivor* on television. I do not talk now so that she can decompress from the day.

9:00 PM ~ Sweetie watches a bit more television while I fix her a bedtime snack. I hand-feed her grapes followed by her favorite chocolate cake. I then give her a much needed foot rub as she channel surfs. She rubs my hair sweetly.

10:00 PM ~ I put the dogs to bed as my Sweetie gets ready for, then crawls into, bed. I prepare for the night ahead myself. I brush my teeth, fix my hair and touch up my face. Next, I spray on some perfume and head upstairs....

Dim the lights....

Turn on some music...

Do a strip-tease...

Crawl in bed beside my lover...

Give her a much-needed back rub....

Feel her relax....

Hear her even breathing...

Know she fell asleep....

Groan inwardly so as not to awaken her...

Feel a little let down that I didn't even get to start reading *Last Train* because I know that I would have gotten laid if I had...

Lie down beside her and finally fall asleep...

❧ ❧ ❧ ❧

Addendum

While reading the first draft of this fine story over breakfast, Sweetie fell to the floor with her eyes rolled back in her head and had to be rushed to the emergency room. I had quite a scare. The doctor explained to me that the simple procedure he had to do in order to remove my loves eyes out of the top of her head would leave no lasting effects. I do believe he called her illness "thatstorywasaloadofshititis". Hruummppphhh....I get no respect! Surely everyone KNOWS that my day really, truly is just like I described...really it is...I promise...!

Blooming Idiots...The Both of Them

"What's a mother for but to suffer?"
~Erma Bombeck

Sweetie and I were almost kicked out of a Totally Healthy Food store once. Turns out that hallowed bastion of health food, organic produce, and vitamins doesn't look too kindly on child abandonment. Allow me to explain.

My twenty-one-year-old son, Buddy, was in town visiting from Los Angeles and I was eager for him to get to know Sweetie better. When I came out to him, he'd made a few crude jokes, asked some embarrassing questions, and then said, "Who cares, Mom, as long as you are happy?"

I was glad that he had been so supportive. This meant the world to me. I cried a bit with the warmth of his approval. Of all my three kids, he's always been the most open. He is an actor. They tend to accept differences in others more easily. Even though Buddy and Sweetie couldn't have been more different - him being a right-brained creative type and her a left-brained black-and-white type - they seemed to click right from the start. I was thrilled. Little did I know what I was in for.

As we headed into Totally Healthy Food to pick up some provisions for dinner and some probiotics for my recurring urinary tract infections, I was enjoying watching them getting to know each other. Maybe she would be a great stepmom after all. This felt great. It felt like family. It was quickly becoming *our* family.

Then I opened my big mouth.

Rows of flowers lined the store's entryway, kaleidoscopic bursts of color, and their stems bending under the cool blow of the air conditioner. I had always adored flowers. When Sweetie and I began dating, she often bought me tulips. My ex-husband never had. It was as if she knew what I wanted without asking. From the moment we met she knew me. In the beginning, that scared me. Sweetie just went with it. The flowers that she bought me had come to signify her love, so, of course, I loved them all the more.

"Look at the cut hydrangeas, guys. Aren't they beautiful?" I asked, admiring the lacy blue bouquets as I debated buying some. "Wouldn't they look great on the entryway table?"

The two of them seemed to be ignoring me. They were busy chatting up a storm and laughing. They were fast friends. I should have been thankful. But they were acting as if I wasn't even there.

"Um, hello?" I said, trying to get them to listen. "Did you see how lovely these…"

"Flowers, right," Sweetie muttered, engrossed in their conversation.

"We see them, mom," Buddy groaned and went back to gabbing with her covertly.

They sauntered off together, and I hurried to catch up thinking, *Just you wait, Sweetie.*

My son had always been quite a practical joker, willing to do anything for a laugh. From the time he was a small boy, he had developed many alter egos that would appear in the most inconvenient and embarrassing of places. He had excelled at sports, but would occasionally run out onto the field or court with very thick (borrowed) glasses, slicked-back hair, and socks pulled up to his knees, acting for all the world like he did not even know what a ball was. Buddy would also burst into song in the middle of class, for no reason, which got him into trouble on many occasions, especially when he chose to sing Adam Sandler's "Hanukkah Song" at the top of his lungs just to entertain his Jewish friends in English. He has a persona for everything and is not afraid to use them for his own amusement. Actually it is a great source of pride for him. Shit, I just realized that he inherited that from me! Sweetie, on the other hand, is quiet. She works a corporate job. Her world before me was basically normal. Things were in their place. The toilet paper came off the spool the right way. It was quiet in her house. Her world after me was oh, so very different! Stuff has a place but is rarely ever in it. We have toilet paper and most times it rolls the "correct" way. It is never quiet or boring. I make her crazy on a daily basis. She tells me this. I smile. Widely.

We continued on through the store, me pushing the cart, them giggling and leaving the work to me. I was looking at the produce and thinking about what to have for dinner when out of the blue Buddy began to juggle grapefruits. He was now trying to get a rise out of me and break Sweetie in to his public antics. I rolled my eyes. I was used to this. Sweetie, however, started to look a little nervous at the direction the shopping trip was suddenly taking.

"Buddy, put those grapefruits down now," I said.

Sweetie looked around to see who else might be looking. The produce section was empty, a rarity for

Totally Healthy Food, so Buddy took his chance to really put on a show for me and Sweetie. But I wasn't laughing. I knew this could only escalate. Sweetie was grinning a bit since no one was around. *Your time is coming Sweetie*, I thought. *Just you wait.*

"Those are some good looking grapefruits. They are just ripe for juggling," Sweetie joked, taking his side.

"However, they are not as good looking as those resplendent flowers that were in the front of the store. Man, those were some beauties. Did you see them Momma?" Buddy chimed in sarcastically. He had a grin that could melt my heart and infuriate me at the same time.

"You two are just freaking hilarious," I retorted and pushed our shopping cart onward toward the tomatoes.

Sweetie couldn't help but get in one last jab. "There were flowers in the front of the store? I must have missed them. Hey, babe, did you see the flowers? Do you want some? Fresh hydrangeas would look good in the entryway. Really brighten up the place."

Great, I thought. *They're ganging up on me.*

Buddy and Sweetie burst out laughing. Here I'd been worried about them butting heads and now they'd turned into the dynamic duo. What a pair they made. Buddy, standing over six feet tall with striking long red hair wearing orange skinny jeans, a black shirt and scarf, and the much shorter, dark-haired Sweetie in her everyday dyke wardrobe of a gray T-shirt, khaki cargo shorts, and sensible lesbian sandals. I wish someone, besides me, would tell her that gray and khaki do not match. I do not care if "all the other lesbians that I know wear the same thing." I am a lesbian, albeit a fairly feminine one, and I do not wear "IT." I wear black and pink and blue with gray but not khaki. Seriously!

"Y'all behave," I whispered sharply over a neatly stacked stand of pineapples as Buddy added two more grapefruits to his rotation. "Drop those damn grapefruits this instant young man or you're going to get us thrown out of here."

As if on cue, Buddy dropped the grapefruits with a splat. There they lay on the floor in heaps of pulp while one mangled piece of fruit rolled under a display stand.

"Oops, that slipped." Buddy picked up a lone piece of salvageable fruit. "I can't reach that other one. I'm sure they'll find it when it starts to stink though, so it's all good."

"Buddy..." I started.

I decided at this point that Buddy was doing this to initiate Sweetie into step-motherhood. This made me a bit giddy. She was not up for that challenge. I was quite sure of it.

"You told him to drop the grapefruits and he did what you said. You can't be mad at him for that," Sweetie quipped. My giddiness started to subside. Was I wrong? Would the two of them be my undoing?

"You two smartasses were meant for each other," I grumbled as I headed off to finish my grocery shopping in peace. I knew that being in a new relationship would have its own trials but I didn't expect this. My own son was turning on me. "Hrruummpphh." We'll see. She'll get hers. I know my kid.

I was halfway to the cereal aisle when I heard Buddy say, "Step right up, folks. This ice tea brand, commonly found in the South, is essential for true iced tea lovers. This real brewed southern style sweet tea taste captures the spirit of gen-u-ine sweet tea. It's now available in tall boy cans. Just pop the top! Plenty of artificial flavors, artificial colors, and preservatives and it only costs one dollar! Grab yours right here."

I peered around the aisle to see him doing an impromptu commercial. It was something he'd done in his improv classes to practice using different accents, making his voice stronger, and getting people's attention. And, boy, did it work. Shoppers began to gather around him. A tall, rather skinny guy with dreads held up two fingers and buddy tossed him two cans which he snatched out of the air and headed off to pay for. Then a quite cute dark haired girl with several piercings edged her way to the front of the growing crowd to ask for a can of tea and to slip Buddy her phone number. He accepted it with a sly wink. Next up was a bleached blonde mom in a low-cut red tank top. She was not much younger than me and she was trying to flash her boobs at my son. Really? I jumped in front of her and she elbowed me to the side and told me to wait my turn. I pushed this kid from my vagina and she was going to tell me to wait my turn? I think not. Bleached blonde bimbo went down quick and easy. Don't mess with momma!

Embarrassing as all this was, I knew what he was up to and that once he was on a roll, there was no stopping him. "If you buy three cans, you will also get a free bunch of fresh hydrangeas. Come on now, don't be shy."

I screeched, "Buddy, shut up about those hydran..."

"You mean these?" Sweetie interrupted, coming up from behind me. She was holding high a bunch of bright blue flowers that she had grabbed from the display cart, getting in on the act. This was so out of character for her. Had she lost her mind? Did she not realize that she was feeding the gremlins? Outnumbered and annoyed, I stared daggers at them.

"I hate you both," I declared quite loudly. "I am going to stab y'all in the neck with the stems of those damned flowers." My voice trailed off into a wail.

The crowd started to dissipate. They realized that there was more than selling tea going on here. I am quite sure that they thought that I was bat-shit crazy and they were slinking off quietly in fear for their lives.

"Mom, what do you have against these posies?" Buddy asked with a glimmer in his eye. "What did they ever do to you?"

"Would you prefer tulips?" Sweetie asked oh so sweetly, whipping out a bouquet with her other hand. "These are quite lovely. I can't believe that you didn't notice them when we first came in."

"Put those damn flowers down now," I shrieked. "I do not want any stupid flowers. I want to get my probiotics and go home so that I can get away from the two of you."

Vociferous laughter bubbled out of my two tormentors. I stomped off toward the homeopathic remedies. Visions of murder and mayhem danced in my head. I wanted to kill two of the people that I loved most in the world. While I was thinking of what part of the body to bury a knife in to do the most damage, an older man in a pink golf shirt approached and tapped me on the shoulder. I nearly jumped out of my skin. I thought that he could read my mind and that I was going to get busted for having murderous visions. I had images of being put in jail with Crazy Eyes from *Orange is the New Black.* In those imaginings she was chasing me around with every imaginable flower, telling me that she loved me and about every twenty-five feet she would stop to pee like she was marking her territory. The man tapped me again and I yelled frantically, "Please don't pee anymore!"

He looked at me strangely and said, "Ma'am, I believe you dropped this bouquet. Those two people back there said they belonged to you. They are quite lovely and would look delightful in a dining room."

Crazy Eyes be damned. I'm going to jail because I. AM. GOING. TO. KILL. THOSE. TWO!

I turned to glare at the two of them and Buddy headed off to find something else to amuse himself with. Sweetie, however, looked a tiny bit contrite. She walked up to me just in time to hear me mutter something about stabbing both of them through the necks, in their sleep, with the stems of the damned hydrangeas. Sweetie chuckled at this. Then she saw my eyes.

"I will kill you right here. I promise I will. I will step right over your lifeless body with a smile if you are not very careful. Now, do you want steaks or kabobs for dinner?"

"Uh, whatever you want, babe," she acquiesced rather timidly.

I went back to the meat counter and grabbed some filet mignons from a rather nervous looking butcher then stormed toward the front of the store. Sweetie followed, snorting a bit under her breath. At that point I heard a very loud, very Irish sounding voice coming from somewhere off to the right side of me. I knew that voice. It then registered that my son had decided to become one of his many alter-egos. Sweetie did not seem to hear him. Maybe she was just praying that it was not him. I knew better.

"I can't find my mommies," I heard him say loudly. "Can someone please help me?"

I smiled wickedly. I had "been there, done that" many a time. Sweetie had not. It was her turn now. I was just going to enjoy the show. Looking around the store I noticed that others were starting to look around to see where the voice was coming from. Some looked scared. Some looked confused. Some just looked at me and Sweetie since we seemed to be the only same-sex couple in the store and the crazy person who was screaming was doing so about his mommies. Plural. Great!

"Please help me," he continued in his best Irish accent. "I am so scared. Me mommies just disappeared. A boy's best friend is his mother dontcha know?"

A group of little old ladies with hair like Easter eggs and handbags to match, were hunkered around the vitamins and were now glaring at us with venom in their eyes and voices as they began to gossip about who that poor child belonged to. "… To think they'd leave a child."

"…Why…good boy…"

"Call…cops…involved…harrumph!"

"Whatever," I thought. "This could only get better…or worse. But fun either way."

Buddy was getting louder with each sentence.

Sweetie looked at me with trepidation in her eyes. "Is that Buddy?"

"Why yes, I do believe it is," I answered brightly.

"What the hell is he doing?" she muttered through clenched teeth.

"Well, I do believe that he is looking for us dear," I told her.

The lady with the red tank top and big boobs walked by huffing, "I'd never leave him…"

I smacked red tank top lady on the back of the head for good measure, "Pervert!" I chided as she headed to the checkout.

"Mommies!" He shrieked. "Please don't leave me again. I will be good. I promise."

"OH. MY. GOD." Sweetie growled. "What the hell—"

Buddy interrupted, "I didn't mean to set the cat on fire again. It was an accident. It will never happen again. Where are you?" He was building in intensity. His accent was becoming thicker. His voice was becoming louder and seemingly more frightened.

"Why is he doing that?" Sweetie whispered.

With a wicked grin on my face I answered, "For shits and giggles."

"Make him stop. Please!" Sweetie was now begging. Buddy was getting closer and closer to us and she looked panic stricken. It seemed as if everyone in the store was now looking for the moms that belonged to the six-foot-tall, twenty-something-year-old, Irish redhead who was quite obviously a wee bit crazy.

I caught sight of him as he made his way over to an older lady with blue hair. He grabbed her wrinkled arm and began to sob. "Can you please help me find my mommies? There are two of them so they should be easy to spot. One is tall and blonde with a pink streak in her hair and the other is shorter with dark hair. I was a bad boy and they left me, but I know that they are still here. Oh please help me find them."

The lady looked around as surely she was on Candid Camera. When she saw no camera, she turned tail and ran. She sure could move fast for someone that looked to be nearly dead. I laughed. Buddy grinned mischievously. Sweetie grabbed her heart and knelt as if to hide. People had spotted us. We were the only lesbian couple in Totally Healthy Food at the time. Wasn't that just our luck?

Buddy then threw himself at the knees of a harried-looking mother of two rowdy boys with a full cart. Her hair was sticking our every which away. There were stains on her Doobie Brothers T-shirt. Her boys were running amuck. One had snot dripping from both nostrils. She was most definitely not in the mood to play. "Oh, thank God, you are a mommy too. Help me lady. I lost me mommies. Have ya seen them?"

The poor woman hardly blinked. She looked as if her children had put her through something similar to this before. "Hello," she yelped to no one in particular. "Who does this poor boy belong to?" She then noticed Sweetie scrambling like a sand crab to get away. "You! Hey, you, over there crawling down aisle four. I see you. Is this your boy?"

Sweetie turned green. It was time for me to get in on the fun. "Sweetie, he found us. Stand up. You can't get away. He is ours in spite of everything and we need to show him love even when he has his little episodes. The cat was just singed after all. It could have happened to anyone."

Sweetie stood up with a look of total embarrassment on her face. I smiled sweetly as I reached for her hand. Buddy did a slow motion run to us and grabbed us both in a big ol' bear hug.

"Mommies, I am so glad that I found you. I love you both and I love the cat, too. You have to believe that it was just an accident." He bellowed, still in full character.

I reached up to kiss his cheek. Sweetie pulled away and ran for the safety of her truck, leaving me to pay for the groceries. Buddy looked in the direction of the door of the store with a malicious grin on his face. He was trying to decide on his next move. That's when I saw the manager of the store take off after Sweetie.

"Ma'am, you simply can't leave your boy here. You will not be allowed back in the store. Ma'am...."

Decision made, Buddy took that chance to run after Sweetie. "Mom, come back. Please don't leave me again. Come baaaacccckkkk..." I heard as he ran to catch up with Sweetie and the manager.

It was a foot race between the three of them. Somehow Sweetie won. When had she gotten so fast? She jumped in her truck and locked Buddy and the manager out. I could see her hitting her head on the steering wheel as the manager yelled at the rolled up window and Buddy tried to pry open the door. What a scene the three of them were making in the parking lot.

As I waited in line, the giggles set in. After I finally composed myself, I reflected over what had just happened and realized that patience pays off and life is good. I smirked happily and grabbed a bouquet of hydrangeas that someone had left close to the checkout thinking that they would be the exclamation point on today's fun little shopping trip. Life is very, very good!

Real Dykes Don't Vajazzle...Or, Do They?

"Sex is funny and love is serious."
~Steven Jenkins

While doing some cleaning in the bedroom, I got sidetracked...as usual...and decided to see what Sweetie and I have in "the" nightstand drawer. You know the drawer I mean...ummm hmmm...**that one**. It had been a while since we had dipped in there and there was a very interesting assortment, I must admit. The first thing that I pulled out was candy booby tassels! It was close to lunch time so I ate a few as I perused the rest of the drawer. Next was an issue of a high-end beauty magazine with a young Hollywood starlet on the cover with a story about "Bad Girl Sex." I must admit, it was her pert ta-tas that made me buy the magazine. Not the "12 moves that will show your REALLY naughty side." I didn't really need any help with that. Underneath the magazine was more candy tassels! These booby tassels are made out of the same candy as those candy necklaces that you loved as a kid. Good Lord, if we dip in the drawer much Sweetie is going to become diabetic!

(**Note to self:** Look for booby tassels that are sugar-free or made out of healthy things like peanuts or carrots or something.)

After that came seventeen candles and a blindfold

in a pink bag. Hmmm…not sure what all that was meant for…but it may be worth revisiting!

Then there was a coupon book. It looked interesting! **Wake me up with morning sex before work.** YES! I like the mornings. Mornings are good…as are afternoons and evenings and nights and well…anytime! Don't judge. I may be getting older but I ain't dead. **Let's get sweaty and have sex in an overheated room.** Not so much. I sweat like a pig…yeah, yeah; I know pigs don't sweat…whatever… Sweating is not attractive on me. Trash that one! **Pick something delicious from the fridge and eat it off my body.** HECK YEAH BABY, make it chocolate, or pizza, or pickles. Oh hell who cares, you got a deal! **Talk dirty to me on the phone.** Great, just what I want all the ladies at Sweetie's office to hear…and I'd get the giggles anyway…I am a giggler! Wonder if dirty text messages count?

Moving on. "Yummy Licks" Warming Liquid in cherry flavor. I can't resist…I take a little nip…not so much cherry flavored as ummm…icky cotton candy that is way past the time it should be eaten. It did warm up quite nicely though. That works for me! A keeper.

Then there were six bottles of massage oil in various scents…one made by "Erotic Bitch"…alrighty then! That's a name ya won't soon forget. By the way, did I mention before that Sweetie loves her a massage? I should also mention that said massage usually puts her right to sleep so it happens, in her words, "not often enough." Whatever!

A feather. That's mine. I love it. 'Nuff said!

A giant set of dice came next. One with body parts such as "face", "chest", "legs" and "surprise" on it. The other had directives such as "Massage my"

(Sweetie's fave...go figure), "Kiss my," "Tickle my" and, again, "Surprise" (my fave...not really a "surprise" there huh?).

There is also a book of short stories entitled "Elemental Passions Volume 1: Earth, Air, Fire, Water, Spirit" by Rhavensfyre. This is very informative, educational and enlightening bedtime reading just in case you are wondering. Kinda goes with the instructive and illuminating television we watch in bed on occasion!

I discovered other fun paraphernalia and toys... heee-heee...Sweetie hates when I use the word "toys"... it makes me chuckle though. I just try to avoid "using my words" in these instances. I am very good with hand signals however. I am like a professional air traffic controller when it comes to getting what I want.

There were also more magazines and some of what Sweetie calls "Gossip Rags." OK, I admit, they are mine...all mine! Something caught my eye and I started flipping through an issue of one of the rags. And. There. She. Was. Jennifer Love Hewitt. OH. MY. GOD. She is so pretty. I admit to a tiny little crush on her. I actually got to meet her once when I was in Los Angeles with my son, Buddy. Lordy! Her bosom has a life of its own! Anyway, while reading the article, I came upon some of her "nightstand drawer" secrets... and one stuck out...glaringly! Jennifer has dreamt up "Vajazzling." You know the old bedazzling that we used to do to our jeans and other clothing; when we put all the pretty sparkly jewels on ANYTHING and EVERYTHING! Well, it is the same thing except she puts the little jewels on her vajayjay...or rather, she has a lady come in to do it for her! A LADY. COMES IN. AND PUTS JEWELS...ON. HER. VAJAYJAY! Who wants THAT job? Umm...Me...Duh! But, how does one get into that line of work? Are there classes? How would it be listed in the phone book? What would your job title and description be? Are there many jobs available for "vajazzlers?" Does it pay well and are there benefits aside from the very obvious ones?

I did do a bit of research and "Love," as she is known to her friends, does NOT use the Bedazzler machine thingy that punched holes...thank the dear Lord! She uses the little pre-glued jewels. Now, I realize that it may be cute to dazzle up the old vajayjay, but is it safe? And, I do not mean safe for the person being vajazzled but for the person that will be ummmm... reaping the benefits of the vajazzilation. I mean, seriously, I have heard an old joke about "that thing has teeth"...but it could really feel like it did with bunches of jewels glued all around, over, and inside... "ewwww"...just no!

I have decided that in the interest of research for all of my fellow lesbian sisters, I will volunteer to add the jewels to our nightstand drawer of tricks and let everyone know how it works out. I am willing to step forward and be vajazzled. To allow tiny little gems of varying shades to be placed in lovely shapes around my tweeter. I know that everyone will be thinking how unselfish I am and how grateful that I am willing to do this for the advancement of *my people*. I offer thanks! Thanks to everyone for realizing how much I am willing to give to the lesbian, heck the whole female, community. To the world even.

I decided to go forth. Go forth to stock up on pre-glued jewels of various sizes and colors for Sweetie's pleasure. I will be vajazzled and present myself and my womanhood in all of its vajazzled glory to my own "Love" as a gift. A dazzling, sparkly, vivid gift.

I called Sweetie to tell her what I had discovered, where I was going, and that I felt that it was now my civic duty to bring this exciting new activity to the lesbian community much as Jennifer Love Hewitt brought it to the heterosexual community. Sweetie, however, did not necessarily feel the way that I do. I do believe her words were something like, "I just don't know what is wrong with you. You are a crazy woman. Are you taking your meds because you really should be!"

I, however, was not to be deterred. Meds my ass! Off I headed to town to purchase some gorgeous, vivid, colorful, pre-pasted jewels for my tweeter so that Sweetie and I could do our part for «The ALV» aka "The Advancement of Lesbian Vajazzling." (I just made that name up. I'm smart like that. Hold your applause please...) At least I know that it is my duty to share with my sister-lesbians the things that I find intriguing, stimulating, fascinating, and interesting. Sweetie just does not understand that yet. But she will. I just know it. Someday... soon. Maybe. Oh, what the hell, until then, I will just hold her hand and lead her happily (read that as "kicking and screaming") down the path of discovery, whether she wants to travel that path or not. She will do this with me and she will damn well enjoy it!

❧❧❧❧❧

"Turn over here babe and get those drawers off!"

These nine little words began our night of much anticipated "vajazzling." Isn't that romantic? Doesn't that make you want to "vajazzle" someone or get "vajazzled" yourself? It should. Oooooh baby, such sweet, sexy, romantic words. Whatever...it worked for me! So I turned right on over and whipped my panties off and said, "Go for it Sweetie." That's when I noticed that she had put a Breathe Right Strip on her nose. I told you, she's a sexy beast!

Sweetie took the pretty pink and purple jewels that I was holding out to her and started trying to open the packages. Who would have thought that the little gems were packaged in freaking Teflon? Holy cow! It took us both fifteen minutes and a few broken nails to get into them.

*Helpful hint ~ Open gems before beginning said "vajazzling." It will save lots of time.

Once we got the jewels opened, Sweetie gazed at me with a look in her eyes that scared me a little bit. She looked a bit possessed. She was going to do this thing and do it right. I was in trouble! She took the first jewel out and sat back on the bed, looking at my lady bits much as Picasso must have looked at a blank canvas. After about three minutes, she put the teeny-tiny, itty-bitty pink dot right below my belly button and said triumphantly, "Perfect!" I started to feel the giggles well up in my tummy and tried very hard to swallow them down. She was serious about this.

The next gem to be placed was a purple heart. She took a few LONG moments and then pressed it midway between my belly button and my vajayjay. It fell off. She pressed again and asked "Does this hurt?"

"No," I assured her. "It's ok."

"The sticky stuff is not working," she said while pressing harder. "Is it hurting now?"

"Only the part where your thumb is in my APPENDIX!"

"Oh, sorry," she replied while pulling back just a little. "The damn thing won't stick!"

"Use a different one," I begged with a tear running down my cheek.

"But this is the perfect one," she pouted.

"There is another just like it. I am sure it's sticky stuff will work and I won't have to have an *appendectomy*," I screeched at her.

"It's ruined," she said dropping her head into her hands. "It. Is. Just. Ruined. This is the perfect one for the plan I have. If I don't use it, it will all be in vain."

"Then, for Pete's sake, get something that will make it sticky." I beseeched, tears now starting to flow freely down my face.

*Helpful hint ~ Make sure that you check out the sticky level of the jewels before you try using them. Without proper jewel stickiness, you could end up with fingers inside your body in places where God didn't put any holes. You may also lose various body parts and lots of blood. All of these things are decidedly un-sexy.

Sweetie went downstairs to find something to make the perfect purple heart stick while I wiped the tears from my face and the blood from my stomach. Boy this vajazzling was fun. Woo-hoo! I heard Sweetie coming back. Fear wracked my body. She walked in the bedroom with her arms filled with various "sticky makers." She had a jar of honey, some chocolate frosting that she had scraped off the chocolate cake that I made for her several days before, a jar of crunchy peanut butter, a tube of superior glue, some weird gooey, brown substance from the garage that was rather scary looking, and thumbtacks! Good grief, she *was* taking this very seriously. I was way past scared now. I was at the petrified point and heading south fast.

"Honey," I questioned her with fear in my voice. "Can't we just use the other purple heart in the package?

Please."

She glared. I shut up quickly.

She started with the honey. I was so happy that I almost burst into tears. I just knew she would start with the tacks! The honey didn't work very well as the heart just floated around on my stomach. I began to sweat. She tried the chocolate frosting next. It glopped up around the heart and obscured the shape completely. That detracted from the perfectness of her planned pattern so she wiped the heart clean, and then sponged the sweat from my forehead and grabbed the peanut butter. It worked. I did burst into waterworks of relief at that point. She looked victorious. After that, she began to work a bit faster, now a woman on a mission. She had a configuration in her mind and nothing would sway her from it. Somewhere along the way, this had turned into a task for Sweetie! She was bent over my crotch with her strip to breathe right on her nose working with all the intensity of a surgeon doing a liver transplant. I started to laugh. First with just a light chortle then very loudly.

"What is so funny?" she asked.

"You, this, us, everything." I was still giggling.

"This is not funny. I am working hard here. I have to do this right," She countered.

Helpful hint ~ Make sure that you explain to your very black-and-white, task oriented girlfriend that the object of this is FUN! Not a "task to be completed."

Sweetie finished right about then with a flourish. "Look babe! I did it! It is creative and I did it! Wanna see?"

"Oh, yes, baby," I sniggered. "I am dying to see your masterpiece."

"It is a masterpiece," she pouted. She was so not

seeing the humor in this whole thing. She handed me the mirror. She had made a perfect pattern! She was a *Master Vajazzler*!

I started guffawing. I laughed so hard I had to run to the bathroom to keep from peeing on myself. When I returned, Sweetie was sitting in the middle of the bed looking very dejected. "What did I do wrong?" she asked.

"Nothing honey, you did nothing *wrong*! There is no *wrong*. Just look at us...You are sitting in the middle of the bed with a Breathe Right Strip on your nose, sweat pouring from your forehead, hands shaking from being so precise, surrounded by various food products, glue, tacks, and gems. I have blood pouring from my belly, purple and pink jewels sticking to my tummy and tweeter...some with peanut butter...THIS is funny, honey! We are funny. Laugh...HA-HA... C'mon Sweetie," I cajoled.

Helpful hint ~ Remember to laugh! Always!

I saw her shoulders start to shake. *Oh God, did I hurt her feelings?* I wondered with trepidation.

Then I heard a huge belly laugh as she reached up and grabbed me and threw me down on the bed. "So, can I make love to you now baby?" she asked, still chuckling. She really is romantic...and sexy as hell!

"I would love nothing more, Sweetie! But first get these damn sparkly things off of my tweeter! This vajazzling just ain't for us!"

And she did.

Talking Hell! I Prefer Make-Up Sex

"I love being married. It's so great to find that one special person you want to annoy for the rest of your life."
~Rita Rudner

I am a "talker." I like to talk. Scratch that. I *love* to talk. I have always believed that we can solve anything personal, professional, or even bring about world peace simply by having a conversation. I worked with emotionally disturbed kids for many years and always felt that by speaking and listening we could change their lives for the better. I went to school to learn how to bandy words about. Communication is the key. Talking things out is the answer to all of life's problems.

Sweetie thinks talking is overrated. She says it doesn't work and simply makes things worse. Basically, in her words, "talking sucks!" But, after our last argument, she says she is really going to try. For me, she says, she will attempt to sit down and discuss our differences in order to work out any discord that we may discover in our relationship. And there are, and will be, differences and discord, and maybe we should throw some disharmony in there for good measure.

I had all but forgotten this conversation, as I am prone to do. Shoot, I forget to wear a bra more than half the time. Anyway, one morning, Sweetie took notice that I was not my usual chipper self. She realized that I was still a bit depressed from the "quite loud discussion" that we had had the night before. Sweetie does not like the word "fight." I call it as I see it and we had a good ol' knockdown, drag-out argument. Whatever wording helps you sleep I suppose. Anyway, she grabbed me in a bear hug and gave me a big sloppy kiss on the neck, which scared the hell out of me as I thought maybe she was going into seizures or something, and said, "Let's talk, honey. Let's sit down right now and sort this out so that we can go forth and have a glorious day."

What the hell? Who was this woman? I thought with more than a little bit of fear. *But, hey, I'll take it where I can get it.*

"What shall we talk about honey?" I asked sweetly.

"You tell me," she said. "You're the one that looks miserable and I want you to be happy. So, talk! Go ahead. Hit me with it. I'm ready. See, I am talking too. Aren't you proud of me? "

How could I answer her? She was not really having a conversation. She was just throwing out a bunch of sentences. Shit! What should I do? So I did the first thing that came to my mind. I mumbled. "Ummm… errr…well, uh, I…I am not uh, miserable. Uh…aaah… errr…I am just a little upset because nothing was umm…settled last uh…night."

"Ok then," she said. "Let's chat about last night. Go!"

Did she just really say "Go?" That is something that you do at a race. Not in a conversation. Oh shit, damn, hell…What had I started?

"Ummm…OK…Well…you hurt my feelings last night," I said.

"How?"

"You said some things that were hurtful," I told her smartly.

"What?"

"Well...ummm...errr..." I stammered. This went on for quite a while. I was quickly deciding that maybe talking was overrated. Especially when you were talking with someone that only used one-word sentences. But there was no stopping her now. She was on a roll. As we finished one subject, she went right on to another. She had obviously decided to solve all of our problems as well as those of the neighbors, the world, and even global warming. All. In. One. Day. I contemplated how to get out of talking anymore. I told her that everything was hunky-dory. I was superbly happy. I plastered on a smile that rivaled the Joker's from Batman and raised my eyebrows. I looked scary as hell. I did not care. I wanted out of this. NOW! "I promise," I told her "It's all good. I am wonderful. We are wonderful. The world is wonderful! Everyfreakingthing is wonderful! You did it! We did it! We had an extraordinary dialogue. Bully for us!"

"Nope, we are still conversing!" she said proudly. "We are solving life's little problems! This is a good thing!"

Then, the light bulb went on over my head. "But honey, I know how you wanted to go to Home Repair Store to get that...ummm...thing that you wanted to get the other day. The silver looking thing or was it black? Maybe it was red, I can't remember. But you know... the thing. That one that you said you needed." She had said no such thing but I am smart and I know that Home Repair Store is always a good diversion, and she always thinks she needs something from there.

"No, babe, this is more important. We are talking

and that is good." she replied.

Damn. Home Repair Store didn't work. She sounds like a frigging broken record with all that "We are talking and that is blah, blah, blah shit." Now what? So I said with verve, "But you also wanted to go look at TVs for the bedroom. I know that the store that you love that carries all the umm...top brands is having a sale! We can buy a new TV for the bedroom. They have flat screens that...uh...hang on the wall. C'mon, I am superbly cheerful now. Look I'm beaming from ear to ear. You did this. I just want to spend quality time with the love of my life. Let's go get that stupendous television that you have been wanting for so long!"

She looked as if she were considering this. I was thrilled. This chatty stuff had gotten old. I just wanted to get out of the house. Now. I was done with all this jibber-jabber. Maybe the world's problems could not be solved with words. Nor ours either. Not if Sweetie was in charge.

"But babe, I promised that we could talk things out. I want to do this for you," Sweetie said, oh so sweetly.

I looked piercingly into her eyes. Something was way off kilter. I was offering up the TV that she had wanted for so long. She was turning into a zombie. I was now sure of it. I was also starting to feel as if waterboarding would be a kinder torture than what I was going through. So I looked deeply into her eyes and said, "You are the most wonderful woman in the world. How am I so lucky that I am blessed with you? You do anything I ask just to make me happy. I love you. Now, let's go get that television!"

"Okay, honey. If that's what you want, we will go and get the television," she said. "I just want you to be happy."

"Oh, I am more than happy baby," I replied as I ran for the front door with my keys in my hand. I was on cloud nine happy. I was euphoric NOT to have to talk anymore!

The rest of the day was wonderful, though I did keep an eye out for any zombieisms just to be sure. We shopped and laughed and joked and bought a great new TV for the bedroom. When we got home, she mounted the TV on the wall while I cooked dinner. We ate and talked and chatted some more. Then we went up to bed and Sweetie turned to me and said, "Honey, is there anything that we need to talk about?"

I looked tenderly into her eyes and pretended to think about it. "Nope," I said, "From this day forward, I think that good old fashioned make-up sex will do just fine for solving all of life's little problems!"

Thank God, she agreed!

ॐ ॐ ॐ ॐ

Addendum

Moral of the story: Make-up sex is, more often than not, considerably preferable to talking!

We Have the "Stinky Kids" in Class!

"Dogs are not our whole life, but they make our lives whole."
~Roger Caras

Alright, in a word, our pups stink! Now please understand that this comes from a place of motherly love and concern. I am starting to worry that our very large German Shepherd and our very fat Min-Pin are going to have no friends that will play with them and be known as the "stinky kids" in class. Well, they don't really go to a class but you know what I mean.

We try very hard to keep them clean but they just attract mud and dirt and sand and gunk. Did I mention Cricket is a long-haired Shepherd? Very, very long haired. And Juno is a very opinionated, very bitey. (Yes, that is a word. I don't care what my editor says. She has not met my little dog.) Little shit. We tried bathing them in the tub...HA! What a joke. And, the joke was on us! They fought and splashed and jumped and yelped and were miserable. So were we.

Next, we tried bathing them outside with one of us holding while the other washed. Again, HA! They fought and bucked and yelped and as we bathed one, the other tried to rescue her. They are very close and super protective of each other. Sweetie and I took more of a bath than they did. It was actually very funny afterward but not so much during.

After that, we took them to a large, well known store for "smart pets." We left them and skipped happily through the parking lot with instructions to come back in a couple of hours. Oh, how wonderful. Time alone! We went and had lunch and talked and enjoyed the experience. That is, until we walked back in the store to get our sweet, loving, angelic darlings. When we opened the door, we were met with glares. From everyone. Even the other dogs!

"Uh-oh," I muttered. "This cannot be good." Sweetie just looked at me with dread in her eyes. "So, how'd it go," I asked the groomer cheerily, trying to remain positive. That's my job. I am the "forever positive one." It didn't work this time.

For the next fifteen minutes we were lambasted with stories of how our wonderful, beautiful babies terrorized the groomer, the other dogs, and the people on the streets- some in the next state! The groomer told us that they were LOUD and howled when separated. To be fair, we did warn them about the separation issue. She went on to say they bucked and trembled and bit (to be fair to Cricket, Juno was the biter!) and that it took four people to get the job done. We tipped very well and ran out the door knowing that we were no longer welcome in that wonderful establishment.

Finally, in desperation, we called the groomer at our vets. They knew us and our girls. Our vet was even a "sistah." So, surely they would be happy to help. They love us! Again, with sunshine in our hearts we loaded the two dogs, sweet little dickens that they are, in the truck and headed across town. When we walked in, our hearts fell. The groomer weighed about eighty pounds soaking wet...and she would get wet! Very, very wet. By the way, did I mention that Cricket weighs approximately a hundred pounds? And Juno weighs about twenty-one pounds but she has a big-dog complex and is temperamental. We left them there and slunk back to the truck knowing that this was probably not going to end well. We were right. When we returned, with a *big* tip in hand, the groomer had aged about fifteen years, was soaking wet and her hair was standing on end. I had never really seen anyone's hair stand on end before until that day. It was not a pretty sight.

She met us at the door with this question: "Have you ever thought of tying them to a tree and using a water hose?"

"Uh, ummm, errr, nope," Sweetie muttered. We paid very quickly and ran for the door, waving as we went.

We tried several more places before throwing in the towel, literally. So, here we are. We have been banned from everywhere. Poor little sweet babies. They are so misunderstood! They are good girls. Just a bit, ummm, rambunctious...yes, that's a good word. What do we do? Where do we go now? We simply can't let our babies be the "stinky kids" that no one will play with. Do dogs like the shower? Am I feeling lucky? Nope! Guess I'll call Sweetie and see if she can pick up some rope on the way home tonight...

NOT REALLY...I would never tie them to a tree... AH-HA...the pool...

I Smell Like WHAT?

"To stop smelling is to stop breathing; people only really inhale the essence of life when they pass gas."
~Bauvard

While snuggling with Sweetie recently, she nuzzled my neck and inhaled deeply. She then nibbled a bit. I really liked where this was going. She nuzzled further in and inhaled even more intensely. I am a sucker for any neck action. Oh yeah, this was going well!

One more deep inhalation of her breath and she started to murmur to me, "Oh baby, you smell so good."

Yes, I thought and started to **truly** enjoy this.

sniff sniff... she snorted again.

"Baby you smell so good. It is almost indescribable. It takes me back baby. Ohhhh, how it takes me back!" She was really into my neck now, inhaling urgently.

My back arched, opening my neck up even farther for her. I didn't care where it took her back to as long as she did not stop.

"Oh, honey, you smell magnificent. You smell just like...BUTTER CRACKERS!" She whispered huskily.

Really into the moment I replied, "Oh baby you say the swee...EXCUSE ME...I smell like WHAT?"

"Butter crackers," she replied completely seriously.

Feeling the moment slipping away, I stammered,

"ummm...errrr...aaahhhh...HUH? I am supposed to smell like Black Currant Vanilla Sensual Body Mist and you are telling me that I smell like a food group... Not even a food group, a snack! Oh whoopee!" I was absolutely thrilled by her declaration that I belonged to group that was snack food. Yummy!

You should have figured out by now that I am a femme. I take great pride in wearing makeup, smelling good, dressing nicely, if a bit hippie-ish. I go to a high-end bath store for my scents religiously and always use not only their body wash but their lotions and perfumes as well. I love to look good and smell good for my girl, and here she was telling me that I smelled like a cracker. A butter cracker! Have you ever smelled a butter cracker? I have not. I do not know what one smells like. I smell like Black Currant Vanilla *Sensual* Body Mist. Period. *SENSUAL.* Crackers are not sensual; whether they are made with butter or not. Not no way, not no how.

"Hrrummpphh," I snorted, "Thanks babe!"

"Honey," she said. "What is wrong? I don't understand why you are upset."

"Oh really," I said. "You just told me I smelled like FOOD and I am supposed to be happy about that? Ummmm, not so much!"

"But baby, I love to smell butter crackers. I told you that you smelled good. I love how you smell."

By this time I figured she was just backpedaling and trying to suck up. But then I looked at her. She was dead serious. She likes the way I smell, even if it is like butter crackers. Isn't she romantic...well, sorta...in her own way...and, if it gets me neck action, what the hell? I'll bathe in butter crackers from now on. They are cheaper than my perfume anyway.

Opening my neck up to her once again, I whispered, "C'mon baby, smell these butter crackers. You know you like it." And she did, which got me some action. It all worked out for the both of us.

I'm going to try Eau de Pizza tomorrow night. She'll really like that!

Two Lesbians and the Quest for the Elusive Chocolate-Brown Leather Sofa

"You can have anything you want if you want it badly enough. You can be anything you want to be, do anything you set out to accomplish if you hold to that desire with singleness of purpose."
~Abraham Lincoln

Sweetie and I have been on a sofa hunt for the past three months. I shouldn't call it a "hunt." That is much too light a word. I shall call it a quest. A quest is a journey towards a goal. And this has been a journey. Whew, what a journey! I never knew that buying a sofa could be so hard. You see, Sweetie is very, ummm, persnickety. Yes, that is a good word. Persnickety means fussy and particular and that is exactly what she is. She had a list of things that were *musts*. Now, I understand that some things are very important but you have to be a tad flexible. Just a little bit. A teeny-tiny smidge.

Sweetie has a list for everything and "THE LIST" consisted of the following:

Must be real leather. Okay. I get that. We have a dog. A very big dog with a whole lot of long hair. As well as the little dog and a cat. That makes for oodles of hair and several licking tongues which are all detrimental to the micro-fiber that we have at present.

Must be chocolate brown. Hmmm...Okay. Well,

this came about due to the fact that she has a chocolate brown, leather ottoman that she has some sort of deep emotional attachment to. I like the ottoman, but I ain't going to limit myself to certain choices just because of it.

Must be an L-shaped, right-facing sectional. I understand...sorta. Sweetie says she wants to stick with a sectional because she loves to sit beside me and snuggle after a hard day at work. All together now: "AWWWWWWWWWWWWW!" She got me there! And the L-shape/right-facing is because we have a long, skinny living area and our TV has to stay where it is. It is very large, fifty-plus inches. It has its own wall. We have our priorities after all. The television is one of them. *Survivor* and *The Walking Dead* are musts in our house.

No recliners. Sweetie says those are for old people...

Must NOT have nail head trim. Yeah, yeah, whatever. What did nail heads ever do to her anyway?

Must not have contoured seats. Alrighty. This is due to sitting on a couple of sofas that are contoured and if you sit between the seats, wood goes up your butt. Not very comfortable nor does it paint a pretty picture.

No fold-down drink holders. We have dogs. They like to drink. Need I say more?

Armed with "THE LIST," we headed out happily, birds chirping gaily above, holding hands and reveling in the opportunity to make our first big purchase for *our home.* We went to the first store and lucky us, we saw something we liked right away! Then we realized that it was the exact same sofa that we currently had except it was not microfiber. It was *bonded* leather. Well, that wouldn't work. We needed real leather.

"THE LIST" said so. We moved on. We actually hit five furniture stores that day. It was exhausting. Who could have imagined that a few items on a list could totally obliterate every sofa in an entire city?

The next day dawned and again we had hope. Hope that today would be the day that we found our sofa. We headed to the truck clutching "THE LIST," tiny smiles on our faces, still holding hands, birds twittering a bit, still fairly happy. That did not last long. We drove to another city. We searched, we sat on, we lay on and we tried out 342 sofas in six stores that day. We found nothing, nada, nil. GAH!

This continued for the next two weekends. Our smiles were not nearly as bright, we did not hold hands, I shot someone a bird, and used "THE LIST" to wipe a bug off the windshield.

"Honey," I said sweetly while gritting my teeth. "This cannot go on. You have to at least try to compromise on some of the things on "THE LIST."

"But honey, I really *need* those things."

"**YOU. DO. NOT. NEED.** Most of those things dear woman. You just want them. Compromise. Just a bit. Please. For me. For us. For our sanity!"

So, we got "THE LIST" and wiped the bug guts off as best as we could. We went over each item and discussed in detail. The leather was a must. But she would give a bit on the color, just a little. Sweetie even agreed to give up the ottoman if need be. She would probably need to see a therapist for a short time to deal with her withdrawal but would eventually be just fine. She could borrow some of my meds if need be. I am altruistic and would have given her my kidney if she would just relent a bit. She said that she would consider a sofa and love seat if we had to, if I would promise that I would still sit with her *occasionally*. Still no contoured seats, nail head trim, fold-down drink holders, or recliners. This was workable. We certainly would be able to find something now.

Not. So. Much.

Over the next couple of weeks, we hit many more stores and revisited some that we had been to before. We looked online and in magazines. We prayed. Nothing, zero, zilch, zip, zippo, zot! I was ready to take a bright orange corduroy reclining sofa and chair that had nail heads on top of the contoured seats with fold-down drink holders.

"But baby," Sweetie said. "We have red curtains. It won't match!" Did I forget to mention that Sweetie also has a strange attachment to the red curtains in the living and dining areas as well? Well, she does. "They came from Pier1 Imports. They were expensive. They are happy and red." Her opinion.

So what? I could whip up new ones from a couple of old sheets if she would just pick a damn sofa...

❧❧❧❧

Sweetie and I were talking on a Friday night. The sofa hunt/quest was still ongoing. We were discussing "THE LIST"—again—as well as any revisions that we may need to make to it so that we could find a sofa and live *happily ever freaking after*. The discussion was getting heated. Voices were being raised and emotions were boiling over.

"Stop!" I shouted. "How did we get here? What caused us to have to be on this perilous quest for the elusive brown leather sofa in the first place?"

We sat and stared at one another, breathing

hard and thinking back. We were filled with dread that we would never find the obscure sofa and would therefore be forced to sit on the stinky old microfiber one throughout eternity.

"STINKY!" she yelped. "That is why we are on this quest."

And she was right, as *she says* she usually is. Stinky *was* why we were on the quest in the first place. We have, as I have said before, dogs! The dogs are very spoiled. Given that they are hard for us to bathe and we have been banned from many pet stores, groomers and vets in our area, they transfer some of their considerable hair and even more considerable smell onto things, including said stinky sofa.

"Remember, Hun, while we were sitting and watching TV one night, I started sniffing you and I said, 'I smell something. What is it?' Remember?"

"Yes!" I replied and I thought back. I had said back to her, "Well if smells like butter crackers then it is me. Otherwise, I don't know what it is."

"Don't you smell that? Surely you smell that. It is not the smell of butter crackers. It is awful!"

"Then why'd you sniff me?" I screeched. "Do I generally smell awful?"

"No," she replied, "I just wasn't sure where it was coming from. Take a whiff...c'mon, a bigger whiff!"

This is a good place to mention that Sweetie is *always* wanting me to "smell it, see if it is any good. Taste the milk, Hun, I am sure it is not bad yet. Just stick your tongue to it, babe. I am sure that fuzz on bologna is ok." I usually do it before I think...yeah, yeah, I know what you're thinking. *"That's gross!"* I have sons okay? The gross-o-meter went out the window a long time ago! So I whiffed. "Oh my GOD! What is that?

It smells like…uhhhh…aaahhh…gah…**DOG BUTT!"**

"Yes," Sweetie exclaimed triumphantly. "**Dog butt.** That's what it is!" She then looked at me very deliberately and said, "Who smells like dog butt?"

"Not me," I replied with a smirk. "You smelt it first. So it must be you!"

"It is not me," she said indignantly as she started sniffing the air.

I started sniffing too. Nothing was safe. We sniffed each other. We sniffed the beautiful, expensive, red, Pier 1 curtains. We sniffed the dogs (yucky, but still not like dog butt). We sniffed the rug. We sniffed the sofa.

"Blech!" I screamed. "Smell that, smell the sofa. It stinks! *IT* smells like dog butt!"

"I'm not sniffing it," she said. "I don't like to smell things that are gross."

"Thanks honey. Thanks a lot!" I rolled my eyes until I could practically see my brain.

So, it was the sofa that stank. Who knew that smells get trapped into the very core of microfiber? Who woulda thunk it? Who woulda thunk that a stinky big dog, a semi-stinky little dog, and a cat with bad breath sitting on an old brown microfiber sofa would have started us on a journey that could very well be the end of the world as we knew it? A journey that might change who we were forever. A quest. **The Quest.**

That, my friends, was the beginning of the quest for the elusive brown sofa.

ᘛᘉᘉᘊᘊ

Sweetie and I continued our quest for the elusive brown leather sofa the next beautiful Saturday morning.

The birds were silent above us. One swooped down and pooped right on Sweetie's truck. Who knew that birds were so touchy? I only threw a few rocks to quiet them a tiny bit the week before. I did not mean to bean a few of the especially loud ones square above their freaky little beaks! Anyway, Sweetie and I held hands tightly as we walked slowly to the truck, looking much as condemned men must look while walking the "green mile." We were clutching at each other desperately and hanging on for dear life. **"THE NEW AND REVISED LIST"** was tucked firmly inside my pocket. It consisted of the following:

Must be leather. Ok, maybe some bonded leather would not be completely out of the questions if we fell totally in love.

Must be some shade of brown or beige. As long as it sort of matched the chocolate brown leather ottoman we were good with it.

Must be an L-shaped, right-facing sectional, or a sofa and loveseat. Could even be a left-facing sectional and we would "make it work" as they say on Project Runway.

Recliners would be ok if they looked "cool." Whatever...

Could have the dreaded nail head trim. But, only if it was *small* and *unobtrusive.* I do not even know what that means...it's nail head! It is made to be noticed! I am not so sure that this was a big help in narrowing things down...but, hey, what do I know? I do now know that birds can be touchy. That's something, right?

Must not have contoured seats. Sweetie and I were still suckers for comfort. No wood up the ass for us! I am sure there is a joke about a woody in the ass there but I am too tired to care, so make it yourself!

No fold-down drink holders. Still got dogs. Don't wanna share our drinks. Just a personal preference.

Must have character. Wait! That is new. Character? What the hell? What did that even mean? Sweetie said that she would *"know it when she sees it."* Well, what if I don't know *it*? What if I thought I know *it* and *it* ain't really *it*? Oh, man. This was not looking good. I pulled myself together and tried to see the bright side…

"Okay honey, remember what we talked about, remain positive, and *let's go find our sofa!*" I cheered brightly. Have I mentioned that I was a cheerleader in school? Well, I was and I was dang good and I could use that now to keep our spirits up. *"L-E-T-S-G-O… that's the way you spell let's go. Let's go! Hey, hey, let's go…find that sofa!"*

Sweetie looked at me from the corner of her eye. "Shhhhh," she hissed. "Just shhhh! Do not remind me that I am dating a chirpy, cheerful, ex-cheerleader person. Not today. SHHHH!"

Sweetie did not really like cheerleaders before me. Nor did she like chirpy, cheerful people. Maybe she did not particularly like blondes…but hey…we can all change our minds huh? We are women and that's our prerogative right?

"Onward," I cried. "Onward to find a sofa!" And off we went.

We revisited several stores that we had already been to armed with **"THE NEW AND REVISED LIST."** As we entered each of the previously shopped in stores, we noticed that salespeople seemed to just disappear… suddenly. How rude! We were paying customers after all. You would think that they had never had customers with **"A LIST"** before. HRRUUMMPPPHHH! My feelings were a bit bruised but Sweetie just murmured,

"Ahhh fuck 'em! Who needs them anyway?"

"Well we do Sweetie," I answered. "Someone has to write up the order!"

"What order?" She screeched. "We have not found anything yet that would call for an order!"

Then, we went to what we thought was a small furniture store. We had passed on this particular store several times because we thought it was a store that specialized in bedroom furniture. I do not know why we thought that, but we did. Upon entering the store, we saw room upon room of all types of furniture. We were jubilant. They had an entire leather room! That excited me on more than one level. (Wink, wink)

As we were walking to said leather room, a woman came up behind us and said, "May I help you ladies?"

We turned slowly around, afraid that if we moved too quickly we would scare the salesperson away. As our gaydar went off, there she was. *OUR* salesperson! A lesbian, just for us. Woot, woot, she would surely be able to help.

"Leather," I whispered hoarsely. "Can you please take us to the leather?"

Sweetie looked as if she would pass right on out. You could see the relief on her face. Surely this lovely lesbian lady in front of us would show us what we had been searching for forever.

"Come right this way ladies," she said. "I can show you a few things."

"We have "**A LIST**," I told her with slight trepidation.

"Oh that is no problem. I can help you," she promised.

"I love you," I breathed wistfully.

"Excuse me?"

"Just show us what you got," Sweetie told her.

We saw it quickly. **The. Sofa.** It had pretty much everything on **"THE NEW AND REVISED LIST"**

Chocolate brown ~ check.

Must be an L-shaped, right-facing sectional ~ check.

Cool-looking recliners ~ check.

No contoured seats ~ check.

Character ~ check. *It* did have character…I saw *it!*

No drink holders ~ *Damn*, I thought when I saw the drink holders.

"No problem," our lovely lady lesbian salesperson told us. "We can take those out. Come with me and I'll show you what it looks like without them. We have it in the back."

I realized then that she was a goddess and that I DID love her…just a little.

We walked happily, gaily, merrily back to see **The Sofa**. It was beautiful. The heavens opened up and I actually saw Angels singing the Hallelujah Chorus! What a moment. Then it hit me. It was too large. It had to be. This was too easy.

"Sweetie, is this wonderful, beautiful, amazing, chocolate brown leather, right-facing sectional too large?" I asked with trepidation.

"Oh no honey," She replied. "This wonderful, beautiful, amazing, chocolate brown leather, right-facing sectional is perfection."

"Measure it," I pleaded. "For me, please, just measure it."

So Sweetie and our lovely lesbian lady salesperson measured. "This lovely sofa is 8 feet 8 inches by 8 feet 8 inches." The salesperson intoned. "Does that work for you?"

"Perfect," replied Sweetie. "Simple flawlessness!"

And we embraced while crying and thanking God that we had been sent a lovely lady lesbian salesperson to help us.

We walked victoriously to the cashier, paid and set up delivery for the next day. We were beyond excited. It was only seven o'clock. We had the whole night ahead of us. We could do whatever we wanted.

"Let's go pick out a *paint color,*" Sweetie said. "Let's just do it right and paint the whole living/dining area before it comes tomorrow."

I just gulped loudly and as I heard the birds outside the store start twittering mockingly. They must have some sort of communication system between them, bird to bird. I fell to the ground in a silent faint of desperation.

≈≈≈≈

I stirred and started to try to open my eyes. All I could really remember was Sweetie saying something about picking out paint color for the living/dining area so that we could paint the entire area that night. Surely she was just joking. Surely she knew that picking out a paint color that we both agreed on could take at least two weeks if we both held true to form as we did while searching for the sofa. She must have realized that it would take us more than one night to paint that whole section. Surely she had not totally lost her freaking mind! I squinted my eyes with anxiety. I was fearful that we would be heading to the paint store yet hopeful that we would be going home to discuss our new purchase. I was praying that I had passed out due to the rush of having finally found The Sofa, not from the horrible reality that we may have to embark on another expedition in order to find paint. I opened my eyes fully. We were sitting in the parking lot of Home Repair Store! As I slipped delicately onto the floorboard, I felt my eyes roll back in my head again and I slept.

When I awoke this time I could hear Sweetie blathering on about "helping a 'sistah' out and finally finding a sofa all at the same time."

"Huh," I said. "You helped your sister? When? What with? And are we really in the parking lot of Home Repair Store?"

"Well, it's about time you woke up. What a strange time of the day to take a nap, babe. We are at Home Repair Store, yes. We are here to pick out paint. Hey, you are not going back to sleep are you? You have had two naps today and that is quite enough." She replied smartly.

"No, I am not going 'back to sleep,' *honey*," I said. "Did you say something about your sister?"

She looked at me with either pity or love in her eyes, (sometimes it's hard to tell them apart), and said, "No, I said that I felt good that we were able to help a 'sistah' out. You know, a 'sistah.' Another lesbian. We girls must stick together so it is always good to help a 'sistah' out," she explained.

"Aaaah I remember now," I replied. "Okay, so we did a good thing huh? Cool. But, Sweetie, are you sure our 'sistah' measured right? I am still worried that The Sofa is too large for the living room."

"Oh, my dear sweet love. A 'sistah' *knows* how to use a tape measure," she said reassuringly while patting my hand. "Now let's go pick out some paint!"

I rolled slowly out the door from my spot on the floorboard while wiping the dirt and spit from my face.

We walked into Home Repair Store. Sweetie had the look of a child about to be loosed in a candy store with $100.00 to spend. I, on the other hand, had the look of a frightened cow being led to slaughter. We headed to the paint aisle and she looked at all the color swatches and with a flourish swept her hand over the area and said, "You pick. Whatever you want, we will get."

I call bullshit! Sweetie does not give up complete control on anything. No sireee. Ain't happening. Not me. Nuh uhhh. Not a snowball's chance in hell. But I looked at her and she seemed so sincere. Maybe I was still a little out of it from the fainting spells. I think I must have hit my head on the door handle and it was making me suffer delusions. So, I said "Okay. If you are sure..."

"Why yes, honey. Whatever your heart desires... as long as it is not purple or orange or too bright or too dark or too beige or..."

"I got it," I yelped. "Please help me to pick out a color, Sweetie. Your opinion is valuable and desired." As I said before...bullshit!

"Well, remember, you insisted," She shot back.

So we looked and debated and looked some more. We finally found just the right shade of beige. It only took an hour. We purchased the paint, some rollers, some plastic, some tape, a few feet of cable ("you can never have too much cable, babe"), and a circular saw (I don't know ~ I just smiled) and headed home. Once there, we immediately got busy. The Sofa was coming tomorrow after all, and it was already after eight. We lay out plastic, gathered our supplies, I poured me a drink, and we began. Sweetie started "cutting in" and I watched her and drank my Sex on the Beach.

"Are you actually going to let me paint this time

or am I just going to sit and watch like I usually do?"
See, Sweetie likes things to be done the "right way,"
which is loosely translated as "her way." She usually
will let me help only in places that can't be seen by the
general public.

"This is our home. You may help paint," she
answered magnanimously. "First however, we must
move most of the stinky microfiber sofa outside. You
can help with that too."

I could help? Little ol' me? Paint? Move the sofa?
How exciting! So, I helped Sweetie move two-thirds of
the sofa out onto the driveway. "Goodbye, dear sofa,"
I chanted in a sing-song voice. "We shall miss thee."
We left the other third for us to sit on until The Sofa
arrived.

The work began. We painted…together. Sweetie
took the trim and baseboards and I took the walls. It
was good. I was singing loudly, "A whole new world…"
We were working together and Sweetie still had all her
hair! As I was standing up on the ladder, I noticed that
the area that the new sofa was going in seemed much
smaller than the actual sofa was.

"Sweetie, I do believe that you should call the
lovely lesbian lady salesperson and have her re-measure
The Sofa. I am sure it is too large for the space we have,"
I said with a bit of dread.

"Oh, you are being such a worry wart. It will fit.
'Sistah-girl' measured it and said it would fit so it will."

"Call her please. For me," I begged.

So she did. The lovely lesbian lady "sistah" said
that she measured again and that the measurements
"had not changed…haha." Who knew that she had a
sense of humor too?

We worked through the night, literally! When we

finally fell into bed, exhausted, we heard a heavy rain falling. We laughed merrily. The old stinky sofa was getting a bath. HA, it needed one. We laughed harder as we fell off to sleep.

The living room looked lovely the next morning when we awoke. The subtle color was just right. We began the wait for The Sofa. When the truck drove up, we clapped, danced a happy dance then hugged it out.

"It is here, babe. The Sofa is finally here. No more stinky old microfiber. We have lovely chocolate brown leather!"

The delivery people rang the doorbell. I swung open the door and there, on the porch, were several parts of our new Sofa! It was freakishly huge! Gigantic. Massive. Gargantuan. Colossal. Big...too big...I slumped to the floor...another "nap" was in order.

When I woke up. Sweetie and the delivery men were trying to fit the massive Sofa into the minuscule place that was supposed to be its home. They were stepping kindly over and around me. So very considerate of them... They were trying configuration after configuration. It was too large. Just as I had said. Whoo hooo...I was finally right! Damn, why did it have to be *this* time?

"Measure it," I said from my place on the floor. "Get the damned measuring tape and measure it!"

Sweetie looked at me with murder in her eyes. "The lovely lady lesbian salesperson said it was 8 feet 8 inches by 8 feet 8 inches so that is what it measures!"

"MEASURE IT NOW!!!" I was no longer feeling love for my "sistah." There was a dark cold abhorrence settling in the recesses of my heart! "NOWWWW!"

So my dear, wonderful sweetie got the tape, handed one end to me and we measured. The Sofa was

10 feet 6 inches by 12 feet. "Sistah" did not know how to use a tape measure. Or she was a liar. Maybe she had bad eyes. Perhaps a brain injury that affected her measuring ability. Maybe she was not even a "sistah." Who really knew? I just knew that The Sofa was now the sofa that would not fit.

"*Take it back!*" Sweetie hissed with venom in her voice, much as the queen says "off with their heads," in Alice in Wonderland. And they did. ...*the sofa that would not fit* rolled away with no fanfare. Sweetie and I looked at each with misery in our eyes.

I looked down at our old stinky microfiber sofa and said "Hello, dear old sofa. At least we still have you."

"Babe," Sweetie interjected with exasperation, "we do not have the dear old stinky microfiber sofa. At least not two-thirds of it. It rained last night, remember? It is wet and gross and nasty. We have one-third of the sofa and we must now begin the quest anew."

"OH. MY. GOD!"

The blackness that overtook me at that moment was welcomed. As I lost consciousness, I felt something wet hit my face and heard the birds above me laugh with glee. *Birds can't laugh,* was my last thought before I went completely out.

"Seriously, babe, this is not the time for a nap," Sweetie said over her shoulder as she walked into the house. "We have shopping to do!"

༆ ༆ ༇ ༇

...And shopping we did! The next weekend we marched forth with as much verve and dynamism as generals going into battle! The biggest problem with that was that we were, more often than not, on opposing sides. I went into the dreaded "I don't care. I can sit on anything" mode of combat and Sweetie countered with, "YOU have to care and you must have a freaking opinion!" It wasn't that I did not have an opinion. I was just tired…battle-worn…fatigued!

We went into store after store. I saw a bright red corduroy sofa that was absolutely hideous and I announced loudly, "This is the one, Sweetie. This is it! Don't you love it?"

She looked at me for a very long time then said, "Babe that is hideous. Get real."

"But," I shot back. "You told me I had to care and have an opinion and here you go. We should get this one. THAT is my opinion!" Battle-worn I told you.

We continued on. I recalled a lovely leather sectional that we had both liked at Ashley Furniture. It was actually the second place we had looked. We had both vetoed it due to the lighter brown color that it came in. Since THE LIST had been revised, we could take another look and see if we could live with the lighter color.

"Baby, let's go back to Ashley Furniture and look at that one sectional that we liked," I said.

"Aren't we banned from there?" she inquired.

"The ban only lasted for a month. It has been longer than that. We can go back now." I told her proudly.

We marched off to Ashley. When we hiked in, the sales people did not disappear. I felt rejuvenated. They did glare at us in a slightly angry manner but we were not scared. We were here to do battle. We glared at each salesperson in turn, sizing them up. Finally my eyes settled on one woman. I looked at Sweetie and she nodded.

"You, ditzy blonde, we choose you." The ditzy blonde fell to the floor. She cried, begged, and pleaded to no avail. We had chosen her.

"Take us forth into The Battle at Ashley Furniture. We shall prevail!" I proclaimed triumphantly.

"Please," Lily, the ditzy blonde, said. "I am not experienced enough. I am ditzy. I am tired. We have battled before and lost. I am scared to go forth with you two again!"

"Come, dear girl, we are here to buy this time. Victory is assured!" Sweetie guaranteed her.

"No, please, no," she begged. "It is late; I have been here all day. I will be the cause of defeat!"

"Defeat is not an option," I cried. "We have been sitting on one-third of a sofa for over a week while dealing with this fiasco. My legs hurt, my back hurts and I am tired of sitting on top of the dogs. Help us, dear Lily, and you will be rewarded handsomely!"

Lily looked at us with fear in her eyes, "Fine. Just fine…I will help!"

"You shall now be known as General Lily," Sweetie told her. "You will lead us straight into victory. March!"

The three of us fell into line. General Lily in the front, Captain Sweetie behind her, and Private Me pulling up the rear. We were a force to be reckoned with. Shoppers jumped to either side of us, some taking cover behind recliners and beds. Salespeople fainted in fear of being recruited. The managers clapped and hooted victory chants at us. We were in pure combat mode.

We walked straight back to the sectional. It was not light at all. As a matter of fact, the color was very close to a chocolate brown. We sat down. It was über comfortable. No wood up our asses. It was real leather. It had no nail head trim. It was, in a word, perfect!

"Why the hell didn't we buy this in the first place?" Captain Sweetie bellowed.

"We thought it was too light," I answered.

"It is not too light. Something else must be wrong with it," she said as she pulled the seat cushions off and threw them to the ground. "Jump on them Private Me and see if they can withstand wear and tear!"

And, jump I did. I jumped on and wrestled the hell out of those cushions. They were tough! "Help me General Lily. Help me test these cushions!"

General Lily grabbed up a cushion and slapped me in the head with it. "Wow, this is a robust cushion!" We both struggled and fought and waged war on that sofa. General Lily is quite a scrapper. And then she did it. She hit Captain Sweetie, hard. A bit too hard. I felt control of the battle slipping away. General Lily was losing it.

"Pull yourself together General!" I cried. "Victory is at hand but you must not kill the Captain. We need her. She has the money needed to secure triumph."

General Lily settled down. There were tears in her eyes. She was breathing hard. She stood up straight and, chest heaving, said, "Shall I write it up?" What a pro!

We put the sofa back together, walked to the office and "wrote it up." We were triumphant! General Lily then looked at us and announced with a bit of defiance in her voice, "That sofa is not in stock. It will be available for delivery on March 16th!"

"Oh, no, that is two-and-a-half weeks away and we are sitting on one-third of a sofa." I said desperately, "Please General Lily, look again."

"No, that is the soonest we can have it to you."

"We'll take it. We have come this far and fought the good fight," Sweetie interjected. "That sofa is OURS!"

General Lily broke down in tears. She felt the success. The other salespeople broke out fire batons and banners that proclaimed victory and danced around the store. They were all liberated. The other customers called everyone that they knew to tell them of the fight they had just witnessed. The managers gave General Lily a plaque proclaiming her "Salesperson of the Decade" as well as a medal of valor, a purple heart, and a promotion. Aaah, victory truly is sweet.

Sweetie and I went home with our heads held high. We were so proud of this hard won fight. We slept soundly for the first time in months. The birds began to sing again. Life was good. We didn't even mind sharing the one-third sofa for another two-and-a-half weeks.

The two weeks passed quickly. Every night we prayed that nothing would go wrong and that our wonderful, brown leather sofa would show up unscathed and ready for our butts to plop on. And, finally, it did! OUR elusive brown leather sofa was finally home. It was beautiful and comfortable and smelled so good! We were elated. We sat on, jumped on, rolled around on and even fooled around a bit on our wonderful new sofa. We kissed it. We hugged the pillows. We took pictures and emailed them to friends announcing our newest arrival. We posted the pics to Facebook. We even named her Lily in honor of the victorious General.

We had prevailed. We had looked the beast in the eye and defeated it. We had fought The Battle at Ashley Furniture and won. We had bravely endured the quest for the elusive brown sofa and we were victorious!

"So, babe, now that the quest for the elusive

brown sofa is over and we prevailed; where would you like to go on vacation this year."

"NOOOOOOOOOOOOOO," I screamed. "Not that. Not now. It's too soon for another quest." Darkness closed in as I sank back into the wonderful, beautiful, comfortable, sweet smelling, brown and leather sofa and napped…this time for real!

Magical Cooter Spray

"The important thing for you as a mom is to be there for your daughter as a trusted source of information. That is the duty of all parents, to be there for their children."
~Unknown

I am a momma. I love it. I believe that my children are gifts from above. I like gifts. I believe that we can do with gifts as we please. I have chosen to use mine for unconditional love, to keep me young, to give me grandchildren to spoil and send back home. Mostly, though, I use them for my own personal amusement. I am very good at using them for this entertainment. It is enjoyable. I do not feel guilty. They are my kids. I can do with them as I please. Over the years I have embarrassed them for fun and pleasure at will. They have grown to expect it and even look forward to it. I know that because moms just know these things. Ask any mother that you know. She will back me up.

Over the years I have been thrown out of ballgames for offering refs my glasses; kissed my oldest son right smack on the lips in front of a whole gym full of people because he had the nerve to TELL me not to do it; hung my daughter's bra on the antenna of my car right before she and her date (who were both too young to drive) got in for a ride to the movies; and chased that same daughter through a big box store with a pair of XXL granny-panties while yelling, "Honey, look I found your panties, they fell off in the toy department. Here, come put them back on," just as she got the nerve to talk to a crush from school. I told you, I am very good at using them for my own delight. But I digress.

Recently, while shopping in a new baby store with my pregnant daughter, I got the chance amuse myself once again. There are so many wonderful tools in that store to work with. First, I saw a belly casting kit. Oh yeah, this could be good. So I grabbed that sucker and held it high over my head like a football player holding up his MVP trophy at the super bowl.

"Baby, look at this. It is a cast for your boobs and belly so that you can forever be reminded of the gargantuan sizes that they both will reach before you give birth. We must have it!" I said just a bit too loudly. I was a cheerleader. My voice carries. I never needed a megaphone then and I don't to this day.

"Mom, that is not even funny. I don't want to be reminded of how big my boobs are right now, much less when I am nine months along. Just put it down. Now. Walk away. It ain't happening. Nope."

She had a point. She is a little slip of a thing but she has some gigantic boobs already. She has since fifth grade. They have been a great source of hilarity for me. Her, not so much. I can't imagine her at nine months and later while breast feeding. But I wasn't giving up yet. "But Sissy look, it says that it only goes up to a 38DD and you will blow that size out of the water before you squirt little Stephen out. But don't despair. They have more! We can get you two of them. Surely you can get those big ol' boobs of yours in two of the kits. What a memory. Oh, honey, it brings tears to my eyes just thinking about it. We could display it in the nursery so that everyone that comes to see him could partake of the beauty of your belly and boobs and know just how colossal you got in order for him to get here."

"MOM. SHUT. UP. NOW." She stage whispered. "People are starting to look at us."

Oh goody, I thought. *Let the real fun begin.*

We continued on to look at strollers, cribs, clothes, and comforter sets. Nothing there to embarrass her with. Then I went up the aisle with all of the stretch mark cream, vitamin E, and diaper rash ointment. Suddenly the heavens opened up and the Angels began to sing "Hallelujah." There it was. "Fresh Mommy Bottom Mist." Seriously? There is a mist for a mommy's bottom? Oh Happy Day! I grabbed the little bottle up and went in search of my sweet girl who had drifted to a more crowded section of the store. You would think she was trying to get away from me or something.

"Sis," I cried out loudly. "Lookie here what momma found for you. It's cooter spray. How cool is that. You have to have it!"

"Mom," she groaned miserably.

"But baby," I said at full volume. "It is a cooling, soothing cooter mist that helps relieve the pain of postpartum vaginal discomfort and swelling. It helps with episiotomies too. You know, that is when the baby is coming out and you are stretched like a too-small turtleneck on a linebacker and they slide in some scissors and cut you. Right there in your vajayjay. Just snip, snip and out the baby slides. This will help the soreness after that and you will be sore. I should know. I popped out a nine-and-a-half pounder. It kind of looked like a huge Christmas turkey coming out of a toaster oven!"

"MOTHER," She hissed. "That is enough. I don't

need cooter spray. I am not pregnant enough to worry about episiotomies yet. Give me a couple more months. There is time to worry about that later."

She calls me "Mother" when she gets in a "mood." I was guessing that she was now in a mood.

"But it is on SALE. Clearance sale! We can get all five bottles that are left for just $10.00. It is a steal. We must have it all," I replied loudly.

The cashiers were starting to stare. I waved at them. I am from the South and we are very friendly lot.

"SHHHHHH," she admonished.

I was on a roll now. "Oh, my gosh, it also helps with *hemorrhoids*. You will definitely get hemorrhoids. I got hemorrhoids. Want to see? "

Two older ladies on the next aisle over nodded their heads in agreement and one lovely lady with lovely café au lait skin and a baby that looked to be about four months old said, "Amen sister!"

"Oh. God. Mother." she ducked her head. "I do not need cooter spray. Go away."

She was still calling me "Mother." I guess she was still in a mood. Maybe it was because of her pregnancy hormones or something. Most other daughters would be thrilled to have a mom that was so helpful during this trying time in their life. "But Sissy, with the cooter spray, relief is only a spray away. You mist as often as you need it, especially after bath or toilet use. And, let me tell you, you will use the toilet a lot, and it is so gross. Anyway, it's made with all-natural ingredients like antibacterial lavender and cooling peppermint essential oils. You can sit easier and feel better. Just look. We must have all the cooter spray they have. Should I ask if they have any more in the back?"

"Damn it all Momma," she said. "Put the spray in

YOUR buggy. Buy what you have. Do not ask for any more. Do not say another damn word. Just pay for it and let's go."

"Now, now, no need to get all testy. We don't want the baby to learn those nasty words do we? He can hear you from the womb." I said with concern.

"Mother. Shut. Up."

I shook my head sadly at the other mothers who were milling around the store and glancing at me with understanding or maybe fear. Those two emotions look so much alike sometimes. I put the five bottles of "Fresh Mommy Bottom Mist" on the counter. I was willing to buy them for the good of my daughter's cooter. I am very magnanimous. The cashier, who was also very pregnant, rang up my purchase. I wondered if maybe she needed some cooter spray.

"That'll be $10.85 ma'am," the cashier, whose name tag read Candace, said sweetly.

"Okeydokey," I replied. "This is some good stuff. It is for my daughter, who is right over there hiding behind the big giraffe. See her? Isn't she cute? She has some big boobs for someone so tiny huh? I bought this cooter spray for her. I sure don't want her cooter to be all sore and bruised or her hemorrhoids to ache. She is so lucky to have me as a mom so that I can look out for these things. Don't you agree?"

"Ummm...I suppose. Sure. Okay," Candace uttered.

My daughter could take some lessons from this cute little pregnant lady. Maybe Candace's hormones weren't at the crazy stage. Maybe she didn't have a momma who helped her take care of her cooter. I could help her. "Honey, I see you are very pregnant. Do you want one of these bottles of cooter spray?"

"Oh, no thank you. I, uh, already, umm, bought some. But, thank you."

I grabbed up the bag with relish and hollered across the store, "Baby, here is your cooter spray. Don't be embarrassed. Candace the cashier has already bought some too. We all have cooters. We feel your pain."

All I saw was her cute little blonde head disappearing out the automatic door. She could still move very quickly for someone with boobs about the size of honeydew melons. All those sports when she was younger really paid off.

As I ran to catch up I heard her talking to her belly, "Don't worry baby. I'll never do that to you. I am adopted. I have to be. That woman is not your REAL grandmother. She is just some crazy lady. You'll be just fine. I promise."

She didn't mean that. She's just in a mood. I know that because moms just know these things. Ask any mother that you know. She will back me up.

So, We Made It Officially Official... Sort Of!

"Counting time is not so important as making time count."
~James Walker

Sweetie had taken some time off "to get things done." This generally means that I am going to get dirty, sweaty, ill as a hornet, and have paint/oil/or general goopy stuff on me. Other people take vacations. That is not what these are. We do not vacate. We work our asses off. I do not look forward to these times. I am very good at pretending that I do though.

Sweetie: "Do you want to scrub the grout in every part of the house with a toothbrush today?"

Me: "Oh, Sweetie, I'd love to do that...just like I'd like to pluck out my eyeballs with salad tongs." I answered muttering the last part.

Sweetie: "Shall we pressure wash the patio, the screened-in porch, the driveway, and while we are at it, the entire house and maybe the neighbor's houses too so that everything will look uniform on our street.

Me: "Why, of course, Sweetie. We wouldn't want the neighborhood to look skewed. I'm sure it will only take us three days...if we don't sleep at all...or eat or pee...or ..." My words flowed off quietly.

Early in the morning during one of these "off" days, Sweetie came to me and said that we had to go to a notary. I am really good at following directions that don't begin with "let's paint" or "we should build" or "don't you want to lay…" so I simply said "Okay Hun," without asking any questions.

She said, "We have to make this official so you can get on my insurance".

"Huh." I looked at her blankly. "Insurance, what insurance? Who's insurance? What official? Did I miss something? Aren't we going to buy paint or plants or some shit like that?"

"Honey" she said, "I have to take care of you and you do not have health insurance anymore so we have to go sign this paper and make it official so you can get on my insurance. That's my job, to take care of you."

"What paper? What is official? Huh?" I will freely admit that I am a bit slow in the morning… and sometimes in the afternoon…and occasionally in the evening. Actually, I just do not pay attention very often. Just ask Sweetie. She'll tell you! The doctor's call it A.D.D. I call it being a Pisces!

"Honey" she said very slowly for my benefit, "You have to have health insurance and since your other coverage has expired, you can get on mine now! But, we have to sign and notarize a paper for my insurance carrier saying that we are domestic partners."

Well, I don't know why that hit me like a ton of bricks…but it did. We have been living together for over a year. We had discussed this before. I always knew we would do this. But still, I stammered and stuttered and hemmed and hawed and finally spit out, "Oh, Okay, that makes sense. Alrighty then, Ummm… Hmmmm…OK!"

"Well don't look so excited" she said sarcastically, "I am not asking you to cut off a foot or anything."

"Oh Sweetie, I couldn't cut off my foot for you right now. I don't have health insurance!" I replied brightly. I always tend to make really bad jokes when I don't know what else to say. I did not know one's eyes could roll all the way back in the head where one could see their own brain until I saw Sweeties response to my little attempt at humor.

"You are so funny. Just a barrel of laughs. HAHA. So, do you want to do this thing or not?" She asked.

"Yes, babe, I do want to 'do this thing.'" I told her. "I was just caught off guard. That's all. I love you and appreciate your wanting to take care of me." Boy, I was shaking and sweating and trying to say the right thing! Where were my words? Usually they come so easily and sound so right and these sounded so weak. Not really what I wanted to say at all. I wanted to tell her how much she meant to me and how much I loved her and how sweet it was that she wanted to take care of me and make things okay for me. How wonderful she was and how lucky I was to have her. And all that would come out is "I appreciate you." How lame is that?

"Lame...you are so effing lame," I whispered to myself.

"Huh," Sweetie replied. "Did you just call me *lame?*"

"NO, babe," I stammered. "I said "you are such a great dame!' You are wonderful and are just great. A great dame! That's what you are. Now, let's do this thing!"

So, she grabbed her keys and the paper and we ran out the door to get it done. As I came down the steps, I heard: "For fuck's sake! Why me? Why now? Honey, go get your keys, I've got a flat. We will have to take the Jeep."

I ran back in the house and grabbed my keys. For some reason, I looked down and noticed that I had on my dirty old denim shorts from the day before. I also had on the Broncos T-shirt that I had slept in the night before. It was covered in dried paint. I didn't see the point in changing before bed. I just figured we were going to do the same thing when I woke up. I also had on bright pink, sparkly flip-flops. I said it was early didn't I? At least I had combed my hair, which had a bright pink streak in it. I was going to become domestically partnered to the woman I loved with all my heart, in ratty old jeans shorts and a rumpled, paint splattered T-shirt and sparkly flip-flops that matched absolutely nothing except the streak in my hair.

When I went back outside, Sweetie was muttering and cursing and kicking her tire. "Damn, stupid tire… Hell, fire…damnation…fuckity, fuck…" She was on a roll.

Not a good start to domestic partnership, I thought.

"Did you not notice this flat when you were out here earlier?" she asked.

"Ummm…nope. Should I have?" I replied.

"You mean you went right by this tire and did not notice that it was flat?"

"Yep, I mean nope, umm yep…" I stuttered, confused. "I mean, yes, I went right by the tire; and, no, I did not notice the flat."

"Do you ever pay attention to things?" she grumbled.

See, I told you I did not pay attention very often and that Sweetie would tell you that. I know my woman! My woman also knows me. And, for some reason that I don't completely understand, she loves me.

We got in the Jeep and headed to find a notary. I

glanced over at Sweetie and started to chortle. "What is so amusing?" she challenged.

"You have on cargo shorts that are a full size too big and a sweat-soaked hat and a Dallas T-shirt with holes under the arms," I pointed out. "But, at least, your tennis shoes match your outfit!"

"Excuse me?" she asked. "What does that have to do with anything?"

"Well, we are going to get domestically partnered and look how we are dressed. This is just how I always dreamed it would be baby. All my wildest dreams are a'coming true." I drawled.

"Funny girl, you are just so very funny! But, I love you anyway! I really do honey!" she said lovingly. "You have no idea. I must take care of you too. This is my role. It is imperative to me. No matter how we look or what we are wearing."

"I love you too baby. Now, let's find that notary."

We drove in silence, holding hands, looking for the first notary that we saw. I finally spotted one. It also advertised that they "Bought Gold and Silver Here," and "Took Anything of Value for Pawn." Whoop, Whoop! One stop shopping.

"Look Sweetie," I literally screamed. (I do that a lot. It scares the shit out of Sweetie but I can't help it. I am excitable!). "There is one right by the bail bondsman and the Probation Officer. Stop there."

"Are you fucking kidding me?" Sweetie asked. "We are not in the best of neighborhoods. I am not stopping at a notary inside a pawn shop that is by a bail bondsman! And, stop your damn screaming. You scare the hell out of me every time you do that!" (See I told you...)

I looked at her with my big blue eyes pleading,

"But baby, what could be more perfect? Look how we are dressed. How great would it be to stop *here*?" I waved my hand with a flourish.

"OH. MY. GOD. You are serious aren't you?" She asked incredulously.

I was clapping my hands and jumping up and down in my seat by this time. It was the perfect place for us. There was even a shop that sold sub sandwiches two doors down to eat at afterward. Ideal, I tell you!

Sweetie crossed herself though she is not Catholic or even religious for that matter. She then pulled in to our gem of a notary so that we could become domestically partnered. I hopped out with a spring in my step and ran toward the door. That's when I noticed that Sweetie was still in the Jeep. I ran back and opened her door and she glanced over at me and said, "I owe you more. You are worth so much more than this and I swear that one day, you will have it."

"Oh, Sweetie, don't you get it? This is perfect for us right now. It fits us. I'm having a blast! C'mon, let's do this thing."

Sweetie stepped out of the Jeep and slowly made her way toward the Notary/Pawn/Gold & Silver Shop. She was looking around like someone was going to jump out at us with an Uzi at any time. The closer we got though, the more her steps picked up. She was finally getting it...this was funny. This was all us... from the dirty, mismatched clothes, to the flat tire, to the notary in the not so good neighborhood. Somehow adventure and fun found us. Who were we to fight it? She yanked open the door to the Notary/Pawn/Gold & Silver Shop and bellowed, "So, where the hell is the notary? I've got to get domestically partnered and I've got to do it right now before the little woman changes her mind." Then she slapped me on the ass.

The little man behind the counter looked terrified. Sweetie can look quite alarming when she wants to. He yanked that paper out of her hand, gave us a once over, wrinkled his nose a little bit...did I mention that we probably smelled? And, then with little fanfare we were finally legally domestic partners with all of the legal benefits that Sweetie's work provides. Sweetie kissed me a quick hard kiss, punched me on the shoulder and said, "You're all mine now woman." Then, I swear, she wiggled her eyebrows lasciviously at the little old man who practically ran to the back of the store.

We left the store, walked two doors down and had a lovely domestically partnered celebratory lunch of meatball marinara subs with chips. What a lovely morning. What a perfect way to become partners. As we got back in the Jeep, Sweetie turned to look at me with love in her eyes and said, "Well, babe, since we are out why don't we go get a pallet of sod to lay in the back yard?"

"Sure thing, Sweetie. That is just what I wanted to do on our sort of honeymoon. I would love to lay some damn sod instead of getting laid myself..." I began to say in an ever decreasing undertone.

Damn, I love this woman!

Fast-Moving Car
A Totally True Text

Buddy: Hey Mom

Me: Hey Buddy, What's up?

Buddy: Shannon and I broke up.

Me: Oh, Buddy, I am so sorry.

Buddy: Don't be. It was my fault. I am interested in someone else.

Me: Playa! LOL.

Buddy: Oh, God, Mom…you can't use that slang. You are too OLD.

Me: How 'bout this slang? Jerk, I am not too damn OLD! Anyway, how did she take it?

Buddy: Wow, I guess that slang really works… sheesh…She did not take it well!

Me: Really, what happened?

Buddy: Well, she came outside to my car and we talked and she cried a little…no, make that she cried *a lot*. Then she got really, really pissed.

Me: She got pissed? Seriously? That girl farted bunny rabbits! What happened then?

Buddy: Well, then she told me to jump in front of the car that was coming up the street and DIE!

Me: Well, damn! That is harsh. What did you say?

Buddy: I told her that the particular car that was coming up the road was traveling too slow and probably wouldn't do too much damage to me but if she wanted to wait for a faster moving car…

Me: Really, Son...that was your reply...to offer yourself up as a sacrifice? Does that really make sense in your head? Huh? Seriously?

Buddy: Well, Mom, that first car would have barely bumped me and I did feel guilty...

Me: WTF... If I had to choose a car, I'd pick the slow one every time! Did you want to jump in front of a fast-moving car and DIE?

Buddy: Well, no. But I didn't think that through...

Me: Then maybe you should start thinking things through...just a tiny bit...

Buddy: But...ummm...the guilt...I kinda broke her heart...and...

Me: Shut up...Shit happens! But you have to think! OMG!

Buddy: Well...

Me: OH. MY. GOD. Just tell me about the "other woman" before I pull my hair out! Is she nice? More importantly, I guess, is she worth jumping in front of a fast-moving car for?

Buddy: Oh mom, her name is Ansley. She is beautiful. I work with her. And, yes, I would jump in front of a car for her...but I'm rethinking that fast-moving thing...I kinda like living and a fast-moving car may not kill me but it could fuck me up real bad! I don't like pain...

Me: Puss! Maybe you should think of that before you break up with one girl for another...you never know! Shannon was a sweet girl but the fact that she told you to jump in front of a moving car and DIE...well that kinda tells you where you were in that relationship.

Buddy: Yeah, Maybe I should date a "mean girl"... then if she told me to jump in front of a moving car... no surprise there!

Me: True dat, Buddy, true dat!

Buddy: Mom, seriously, DO NOT use slang!

Me: Oh for heaven's sake. Why don't you just jump in front of a car and die!

Buddy: Wow, I see how you are Mom. Didn't have you pegged for a "mean girl."

Me: Make it a fast one, OK?

Buddy: Dang, love you too!

It Took Forty-Ahem Years For That? Damn, What a Waste!

"I don't have a dirty mind, I have a sexy imagination!"
~Unknown

A funny thing happened in bed a while back. Now, for the record, I have been sexually active for many years. Too many years to recount here for fear of my children basically throwing it in my face and making all my lectures to them seem hypocritical. Which, by the way, they basically were. Sorry kids. I had to keep ya'll safe somehow. Anyhoo, I tell you that little tidbit so that you may know that I am not a prude (by a longshot) and I am pretty much up on most all things sexual. I like sex, a lot, and would have it as often as possible (read every single damn day and twice on Sunday) if given the choice. Before I start my little story, I need to let you know if you are easily offended or grossed out or especially if you get jealous about the sex lives of others, you may just want to skip this story because there is a lot to be jealous of here (wink, wink)!

Sweetie and I were in bed "fooling around," "bumping boots," "doing the nasty" (snort), just plain ol' "having sex," or if you are still all dewy eyed and in the throes of a new relationship (gag), "making love." It was good. I mean it was really, toe curling, hair grabbing good! The big "O" had already hit me twice and I was feeling alternately tired, elated, bruised, loved, sleepy, satisfied, and more than a little bit like Jell-O when Sweetie growled, "Can I have some more?" in my ear.

The Energizer Bunny kicked in. I was tired no longer! You see, I have this thing about my ears and Sweetie growling into one of them hit me right where she wanted it to. BAM! Square in the tweeter! I was instantly ready again. "Yeah, baby," I panted, sounding a bit like Austin Powers.

Things progressed pretty quickly from there. Remember, I had already "finished" twice and Sweetie was going all out. She drank a Mountain Dew for dinner and that always hypes her up and makes her pretty much insatiable. I, myself, do not drink Mountain Dew, but it is damn near my favorite drink, if you get my drift.

I was heading straight on toward another orgasm when, out of the blue, things started to change. My toes, which ALWAYS curl in, straightened and spread right the hell out. My knees bent backward (is that even possible?). My eyes began to cross. My hair literally stood on end. My hands, which are usually used to clutch the sheets, grabbed Sweetie by her ears until she looked a bit like Dopey from the Seven Dwarfs and dragged her face close to mine. I looked her dead in her eyes and howled, "DO. NOT. DARE. STOP. WHATEVER. THE. HELL. YOU. ARE. DOING. OR. I. WILL. KILL. YOU. IN. YOUR. SLEEP." (I know, I know…such sweet pillow talk! It's clearly the Southern belle in me). My head then spun around on my shoulders followed by some Romanian swear words and more than a little bit of drool.

Sweetie is a very smart woman and she did not stop what she was doing. I am not sure if it was the

Mountain Dew, her pride or pure fear that kept her going at that point and I did not care. I just knew that whatever was happening to me was most certainly not a regular orgasm. It was like a super-hero orgasm and should have been accompanied by super-hero captions above my head like: "SHAZAM," "POW," "ZOWEE," "DEAR SWEET BABY JESUS PLEASE DON'T STOP," and "ZOINKS." That's how intense it was!

Suddenly, my upper body lifted from the bed then dropped again. HARD. My lower body followed suit but stayed in the up position defying gravity. I felt like I was in *The Exorcist*! I did not care. Then *it* happened. I felt liquid. Liquid that was coming from me. A watery substance was literally spewing from my body. SPEWING! And, the worst thing was that there was a whole hell of a lot of it. "What in the world?" I wondered in a mixture of fear and embarrassment.

Sweetie growled. I screamed. She was elated. I was mortified. My lower body hit the mattress with a thud.

When things calmed down a bit, Sweetie asked with a purr, "Are you okay?"

"Uh, Errrr, Ahhh, I don't know. I think I just peed myself." I replied, wide eyed. "Oh God, I am so sor…"

She interrupted me. "Oh honey," She said soothingly. "You didn't pee yourself."

"What do you mean I didn't pee myself? LOOK!" I screeched in embarrassment pointing to the standing pool all around us. We could have done laps in the bed!

"No babe. It's all good! You just ejacu…" she started

Then it hit me and it was my turn to interrupt. "SHHHH," I jumped in quickly. "I know now. We don't have to talk about it. Or, say it out loud…"

"But, honey," she interjected. "It's a beautiful

thing…"

"LA, LA, LA DEE DA!" I sang with my fingers in my ears.

"Dammit, now, stop that," Sweetie admonished. "Did we make love?"

"Yes," I said feeling a bit shy for some reason. I was never shy about sex.

"Was it good?" she asked.

"HELL YEAH!" I answered loudly this time.

"Any regrets?" She probed.

"Only that it took me forty-ahem-years to figure out that I could do this. Damn! What a waste!"

"It just took me baby," she boasted in a sexy whisper into my ear again.

"Yeah, that's what it was," I agreed. "Now, stop your whispering in my ear. I'm so tired and you know where the ear thing leads!"

"Do you want to do it again?" She wiggled her eyebrow in question.

"YES. YES. YES. OH, YES. But can we wait a day or so? We may need to invest in some goggles or an umbrella or a scuba mask or something. I don't want you drowning or choking or something equally horrendous." My eyes were starting to droop with sleepiness. I was truly satiated. "I don't want to have to call an ambulance to revive you!"

Sweetie grinned, "Well, then, hush up and wiggle on down here to the bottom left corner of the bed. I managed to find a dry spot where we can snuggle before we go to sleep. It's not very big but I think if we spoon…"

"Sheesh. Thanks, Hun. Way to make me feel less self-conscious." Then I grinned at her and backstroked on down into her waiting arms and we slept the night away in the dry spot!

❧❧❧❧

Addendum

For those of you who are jealous of my glorious sex life tale but read it anyway...
Neener, neener, neener!

Paging Dr. House

"There's a fine line between crazy and free spirited and it's usually a prescription."
~Unknown

Oh Dear Lord. I just went to the bathroom with IV pole in hand, attractive green gown gaping open in the back, ass hanging out, bladder screaming, plopped down to pee, felt warm fluid begin to flow over my buttocks, and realized that housekeeping had snuck in like a thief in the night and stuck one of those damned *"Your toilet was sanitized by..."* thingies across my toilet seat! For no good reason. No one else is using my toilet. I'm in a private room. Yuck. I reached around for something to clean my posterior with and whaddayaknow? They may have cleaned my toilet... but they did not clean anywhere else. No washcloths, no soap, nothing. So I made do. I grabbed a handful of tissues reached back and used some of my shampoo from home, wet it in the sink, and washed the old crotch right off. Hmmm, I wonder if this is a good idea for someone with a screaming kidney. At least my cooter is clean. Priorities people!

Anyway I am getting ahead of myself. I have been languishing in the tranquil confines of our friendly neighborhood medical facility for the last five days. I am done. The paint color sucks. The décor sucks. The tiny television sucks. The nasty third shift aide with squeaky Crocs sucks. The food sucks. Basically everything sucks. I am over it. I want out of here!

I was transported to said medical facility early on a Tuesday morning by Sweetie. After writhing in pain and screaming for the better part of Monday night Sweetie *"threw my ass in the truck and took me to the hospital whether I liked it or not."* FYI, I did not like it. I still do not like it. I do not anticipate myself liking it in the foreseeable future.

Sweetie dropped me off at the emergency room door and headed off to work. She does not *"do"* hospitals. I entered the E.R. smiling, much like Heath Ledger's Joker on *Batman*, through my pain. I saw an older gentleman behind the front desk, nodded a "how do you do," grabbed him by the front of his shirt and shrieked, "I WANT DRUGS NOW!"

I have given birth to three children, never accepting medication with any of them even when the pain was intense. One of those children was well over nine pounds. I was stupid then. I am older now and much, much wiser. This wisdom was screaming at me to beg for any kind of narcotic that the lovely hospital people would fill me with in order to stop the pain that was emanating from my kidney area. Screaming and physical threats seemed to be the only ways for me to make the fellow behind the desk understand my needs. I thought that it was working for me until a very unpleasant policeman came up behind me, pried my fingers from around the old geezer's neck and said, "You must follow procedure."

I thought I was.

After "following procedure" with the assistance of the nice policeman, I was checked in and taken back into an emergency cubicle and told to, "wait my turn."

I did not realize then that "wait my turn" meant "We will be back in about three hours…If you are lucky." So much for luck. After several hours and much prodding, poking, and questions by numerous people, a young doctor came in and said, "Well, my gosh, can you please get down off of the ceiling long enough for me to assess your pain level? You also appear to be about the color of a tomato so I think you may have a fever to deal with as well."

"Ya think?" I yelped as I unhooked my nails from the ceiling tiles and slid down the wall.

"Quite possibly," he replied. "We will check that now." He had a nurse jam a thermometer in my mouth at approximately the same time that he karate chopped my right kidney with enough force to break through six concrete blocks. I swallowed the thermometer, screamed a few swear words, and flew right back up to the ceiling, shaking like a leaf on a tree during a hurricane.

"On a scale of one to ten, what would you rate your pain?" he asked.

"Forty-seven," I shrieked. "The pain is at a forty-seven!"

"Well, if you could just cough that thermometer back up, we could get a temp on you and perhaps get you something for the pain," He offered.

I hocked that thing up fast! "104.6. My goodness, you seem to have an infection," said an obviously brilliant nurse that had just popped round the corner.

"DUH."

"Okay, you go pee in this cup while I order up some tests and meds for you and we'll get you fixed right up," The doctor assured me.

"You mean I have to walk? It hurts to walk. It

hurts to pee. I can't do it. I can't, I can't, I really, really can't," I whined like a big ol' baby.

"You want something for the pain then you'll do it," Dr. Meanie demanded.

I moved toward that bathroom like Flo-Jo in her glory days. The pee was back in his hands in 12.2 seconds! I hurt like hell and wanted those drugs ASAP.

He looked at the urine and clicked his tongue and said, "My, my. This is bad. Let me get you some meds ordered." He ordered the nurse to start an IV on his way out the door.

Sheesh…finally!

I lay back and actually felt tears start to roll down my cheeks as the IV was slipped into my vein. I was really hurting badly. My daughter came in about that time and started petting me. She works at the hospital. This is a good thing. People treat you wonderfully when they find out you have family that works there. I looked up into her sweet little face, stroked her cheek, told her how glad I was to see her, and that I loved her dearly, and then I bellowed "MAKE. THEM. GIVE. ME. DRUGS. NOW!"

She looked at me kindly and said, "It is on the way momma. Just hang on."

The doctor came back in, looked me in the eye, and told me that I was not going anywhere. I must stay in the hospital. I was very ill. I begged to differ with him. I wanted an antibiotic and something to stop the pain, and I was going home. A tussle ensued. We argued back and forth. He then pulled out a needle and inserted it into my IV.

Life became beautiful. Warmth surrounded me. I saw **purple**, **blue** and **yellow** flowers growing all around me. I fell in love with the cute little bald doctor.

I wanted to marry him. I found the hospital and all of its inhabitants irresistible. I decided that living here could be an exquisite thing. Dilaudid was my friend.

So this is how I ended up at the hospital, IV pole in hand, attractive green gown gaping open in the back, bladder screaming, with pee across my butt. I blame it on the cute little bald doctor with his blessed hypodermic full of Dilaudid.

𝔰𝔩𝔰𝔩𝔰

I woke up at approximately 7:00 AM on my second day in the hospital. My pain meds had worn off, I really had to pee, and I could feel people standing over me. I opened one eye. There were five people in white coats. I closed that eye quickly. I opened the other eye. On that side there were seven white coats. I closed my eyes tightly. I thought I was dead and these people were the ones that had been chosen to greet me. I didn't know any of them and I was frightened. Was this some sort of cosmic joke? I died and didn't even know the folks that came to get me? What the hell… or maybe heaven?

"Open your eyes, Hun," I heard a female say. "You have been asleep for a while now and we need you to wake up."

I opened them slowly. I was not at all sure if I trusted these people. Sheesh, some of them looked young enough to be going to prom this year. Once my eyes were fully opened, I realized that I had entered a television episode of *House*! You know the show *House*, right? It starred Hugh Laurie and the stunning Olivia Wilde (twitter, pant), among others. Well, right beside me was *Dr. Foreman* in female form. She was Asian and beautiful and very smart and clearly the "leader" of the group. To her right was *Dr. Chase.* He was a younger guy with a cute dimple in his chin who looked like he should be riding a surfboard instead of being stuck in the hospital. Then there was *Dr. Taub,* also in female form. This was not a pretty picture. I was certain she was a great doctor but wow, looking like *Taub* is a strike against you if you are a male! God help you if you are a female. Dr. Cuddy stood at the foot of the bed. She was a beautiful woman, very intense, knew what she was doing and kind. On the other side were, among others, *Wilson, Cameron,* and my favorite of them all *"Thirteen." Thirteen, who was played by the aforementioned Olivia Wilde,* was a beautiful, sensuous, bisexual woman. She was HOT. I was a mixture of scared, agitated, awe-struck, in pain, and sick as hell.

"How are you this morning?" *Dr. Foreman* inquired.

"I feel like shit and hurt intolerably," I answered.

"Where do you hurt?" queried *Cuddy.*

"My lower back," I pointed.

"Here?" probed *Foreman* as she slammed her whole forearm through my back at waist level.

"AAARRRGGGHHH!"

"I'll take that as a yes," *Cameron* said making a mark on his chart.

"Let's get her something for pain and then we will go over symptoms," *Foreman* interjected.

The lovely, beautiful nurse bustled in with a shot that went right into my IV. Flowers bloomed. A rainbow formed in the corner of my room. All of the dear doctors were now wearing tie-dyed lab coats. It was vibrant. I loved my room and all of my new friends

"So, tell me what brought you here," someone

said.

"Sweetie's truck."

"No, what symptoms were you having?"

"Aaaah, pain, lots of pain. High fever. Pain when urinating. Urinating is a peculiar word. HAHA. I like pee-pee better. Don't you *Dr. Thirteen*?" I winked at her.

"Yes, pee-pee is a good word, Hun. Stay with us now. Any other symptoms?" *Thirteen* asked in a sultry voice. I was sure she was flirting.

"Nausea and pain. Did I say pain? You are very, very cute," I informed her.

Dr. Thirteen said, "Thank you. Is that all of your symptoms?"

"Yep, I do believe so. Except for the pain. There is a lot of pain!" I replied. "Where is *Dr. House?*"

"Huh?" several of the residents queried quizzically.

"Oh, so this is a secret. No one knows that you guys and Dr. *House* are here yet. Cool. You can trust me," I stage whispered. "Shhhhh." I locked my lips and threw away the key.

They continued to stand around my bed and go over all of my symptoms in order to try to figure out which tests to order. I felt very important. While they were talking, I had an epiphany. They always check for one disease in particular on *House.* That must be what is wrong with me. They just haven't thought of it yet. Duh!

"*Sarcoidosis!*" I bellowed. "That is what it has to be. It is always that. Just ask *House.* Run the tests! We did it team! Yeah."

Taub looked over at *Wilson* and said, "She is hallucinating. Hit her with the Dilaudid again."

Daisies, roses and butterflies filled my room.

Dr. Thirteen sat down on the chair beside my bed and stroked my hand. "Don't worry Hun," She said. "We'll find out what this is and fix you right up. Then you and I will run away and get married."

Hey people, these are MY medicated memories. Don't be a hater.

~~~~~~~~~~

A few evenings later daughter, Sissy, and I were hanging out in my hospital room watching TV and talking. Face it: there is nothing else to do in the hospital. We were watching "Dancing with the Stars" when all of a sudden this short little man burst into my room with egocentric aplomb. He was followed by two residents that I immediately dubbed Tweedle-Dum and Tweedle-Dee because they looked like bookends. They were Indian so they had very dark skin, hair and eyes. They had these huge smiles plastered on their faces and their dark skin made their über-white teeth emit a glare that was a bit startling to the naked eye. They also had on astonishingly white lab coats. Their perfectly polished shoes, flawlessly ironed and creased pants, and gleaming stethoscopes matched from tip to toe.

I realized that this little man was Dr. House in disguise. I had been right all along! This was my very own episode of *House*. He stalked right up to my TV and turned it off. I actually had my hand on the button on my bedside control so that I could turn it down while still seeing the picture, but he was fast and totally in charge. I immediately knew that he suffered from "Napoleon complex," a condition whereby undersized men compensate for their smallness (wink, wink) by physically, mentally, or emotionally asserting their presence. My daughter and I were taken aback. How could we watch Chad Ochocinco, who definitely does not have "Napoleon complex", and his extremely hot partner, Cheryl Burke, do the salsa? Well, hell. This was bad.

Dr. House whirled toward me and said gruffly, "So, you are sick huh? That's what you think? Well, is it? Speak up girl. What's wrong? Cat got your tongue?"

Tweedle-Dum and Tweedle-Dee looked at me quizzically, heads turning from side to side like our German Shepherd does when she hears a strange noise.

"Ummm," I stammered. "Yes? I believe so. What do *you* think?" Dr. House scared me a bit. His compensation for his smallness was working on me. He was loud and overbearing and acted like he was very much superior. I bought it hook, line and sinker.

He noticed my daughter at that point. She had been trying to climb under the chair for safety. "YOU," He shouted. "Get out. Now! Unless you are sick too. Are you?" My wonderful, sweet, brave daughter shook her head vehemently and bolted from the room like a deer that had been hit with buckshot. So much for her helping me out. Chickenshit!

He whirled back on me and said, "Well, you should know better than anyone if you are sick. Don't you think?"

Tweedle-Dum and Tweedle-Dee nodded as if I were stupid.

"Well, yes, I believe I shou—"

"Do you think your fever broke because you have been here for a week or because you finally got the right antibiotic?" he interrupted vociferously.

I sat up straight and tried to sound as intelligent as possible with basically no sleep, fear running through my veins along with the Dilaudid that had just been shot into my IV. I am not sure it was working for me. I don't think I was thinking or speaking too intelligently. I tried though. I really did! I actually sounded like a simpering boob.

"I believe it was the antibiotic sir. I have had five different antibiotics since I got here on Tuesday. None of them even touched my fever. Within an hour of starting this last antibiotic which you ordered, my fever broke, the chills stopped, my pain lessened…"

"Well, what do you know?" he asked. "Did you go to medical school?"

Tweedle-Dum and Tweedle-Dee looked at each other and smirked.

Assholes! I then stammered on in confusion. "Ummm, well, I know that I felt better after the medicine and that is what you asked. Wasn't it?"

Dr. House walked over to me, leaned down close enough for me to see the spit forming on his tongue and bellowed, "You could have died! Do you know that? Why didn't you come to the hospital sooner?"

Tweedle-Dum and Tweedle-Dee nodded pompously.

I wiped spit from my eyebrow and said, "I don't know why I didn't come sooner. I am not sure if I knew I could have died. I don't think I did. I didn't mean to almost die. I am sorry." I was apologizing to him for being sick and interrupting his day. How did that happen? How did he make me feel guilty for being sick? As I said, I sounded like an idiot.

"Well, you don't need to do this again. Ever. Do you understand?" he said while turning to Tweedle-Dum and Tweedle-Dee. "Now, gentleman, what are your thoughts?"

Tweedle-Dum and Tweedle-Dee looked at one another as if trying to figure out whose turn it was to speak first. "We think she could have died," The shorter one said.

"Yes, and she should have come to the hospital sooner," said the other.

"Yes, yes," said Dr. House. "Exceedingly enlightening. Anything else?"

"She is sick," they chimed in unison. "And, the correct antibiotic finally alleviated her symptoms."

"Spot on," Dr. House said. "You boys are real brainiacs. The face of medicine to come. We should all be scared beyond belief. Blondie here came up with basically the same answers that you two did and she has never even stepped foot in a medical school. Imbeciles!"

House glanced at me and said, "You'll get better if you don't die first so keep your chin up."

"Ummm, thanks. I think. Okay..." I replied shaking my head. I wasn't sure if I was stupid, he was way too smart or the Dilaudid was very, very good.

Dr. House headed out the door with Tweedle-Dum and Tweedle-Dee shuffling along behind him. I heard the taller one say, "I think it could be sarcoidosis!"

"Yes," agreed the shorter one. "She has all of the symptoms."

"No you fools," House said. "She does not have all the symptoms. You both have more symptoms of sarcoidosis than she does. She has bilateral acute pyelonephritis. Do you even know what that is? Maybe you should Google it. God, where is medicine headed? I need ten more of me to work with around here. The world needs thousands more of me to alleviate the suffering of others around the earth. I know best. I am superhuman. I am brilliant, skillful and gifted. I know everything. I am infatuated and obsessed with myself to the exclusion of all others and ruthlessly pursue my own gratification, ambition, and world domination. Some may see me as a narcissist. I see only perfection…"

Then he was gone. I had been privy to his majestic glory. I would be healed now just by having him in my room. Tears started to form in the corners of my eyes. How lucky was I to have just been in his presence? If you believe this part, I feel sorry for you. What really happened is that I threw up a little bit in my mouth while listening to him toot his own horn. LOUDLY! He was an ass, albeit a very intelligent ass. He did figure out what was going on with my kidneys and hopefully fixed them. For this I am forever grateful.

My daughter (the big ol' chicken) quietly snuck back in the room looking around like Elmer Fudd when he's going "wabbit hunting" and flipped on the TV once again, although at a very low volume. Chicken, I tell you! Chad Ochocinco was just beginning to dance. This made her happy. Partner Cheryl was shimmying in a very skimpy dress just as my nurse brought in another shot of the Dilaudid. These things made me happy. We both squealed with delight and settled in to watch the dancing.

ஜ ஜ ஜ ஜ

Seven days later, Sweetie finally got to come and pick me up to take me home. Just as Dr. House predicted, I got better instead of dying first. Yay! When I got to our wonderful house, I literally crawled out of Sweetie's truck and kissed the grass in our front yard. I then went inside and hugged our fur-babies for a very, very long time. I was so very happy to be home, though I did miss my dear, sweet, loving, beautiful Dilaudid. Oh, as well as Dr. House and the delicious hospital food… NOT! But, my kidney was on its way to being healthy and that was what counted in the end. And, I had some great psychedelic memories about Dr. Thirteen to sustain me until I was completely better and beyond.

Electoral College
A Totally True Text Message

Sissy: Mom, how do you get into Electoral College?

Me: Huh?

Sissy: You know, Electoral College. Where you learn all about the candidates and how to vote.

Me: Huh?

Sissy: Mother, I know I am not as political as u or Bubba...or even Buddy for that matter...but I need to learn all the facts so that I can make an intelligent choice when I go to the polls. Lookie Momma, I used a political term..."Go to the polls." See, I can learn what I need to know if I can just go to this Electoral College thing...

Me: I don't understand Sissy...Electoral College?

Sissy: Yes, Mother, That is where you go to learn to vote. Duh! I never got the voting bug but now that I am lobbying for children's and teens' rights, I need to be up on all my facts so I figured Electoral College would be the best way to go.

Me: Are you serious Sis?

Sissy: Yes Mom. Why would I ask if I weren't serious? I have good grades. I am on the Dean's list, several sororities...I am smart...I need to vote and Electoral College is the way to go! So, tell me, how do I get in and where is the nearest one or can I do it online?

Me: Honey, type very slowly so that I can

understand ok?

Sissy: Mother. I. Need. To. Get. Into. Electoral. College. So. That. I. Can. Learn. To. Vote. And. Get. All. The. Facts. About. The. Candidates. How. Do. I Go. About. That?

Me: Sissy, the Electoral College is not a place that you go to learn about candidates or to learn to vote. It is the institution that officially elects the President and Vice President of the United States every four years. The President and Vice President are not elected directly by the voters. Instead, they are elected by "electors" who are chosen by popular vote on a state by state basis.

Sissy: Well, WTF? Why is it called a college?

Me: Sissy, have you been listening to the bullshit that your brothers feed you again?

Sissy: Well..ummm…

Me: Sissy?

Sissy: So, I don't have to go to Electoral College?

Me: No dear, you simply have to register to vote.

Sissy: Gotta go mom. I have 2 calls to make…ass hats…BTW, you had boys why????

Me: For shits and giggles Sissy, for shits and giggles…and it's working out so far :)

Sissy: SHUT. UP.

Me: I love you…(giggle…giggle…really Sissy?)

Sissy: Whatever :(

༄ ༄ ༅ ༅

Totally True Follow-Up Text to Son #1

Me: Seriously, did you boys tell your sister that she had to go to Electoral College?

Bubba: Huh? Who?

Me: Don't who me, Bubba. I know you were in charge of this. This has you written all over it!

Bubba: I don't know what you are talking about…I would never…

Me: I call Bullshit!

Bubba: Oops, gotta go Mom, Sissy is texting and she wants to know where to   send her transcripts to get into Electoral College…ROFLMAO!!!!

Me: BUBBA!!!!

Bubba: :)

❧❧❧❧

Sissy asked that I add a disclaimer stating that she is, in fact, not stupid. She is just gullible and believes every damn thing that her older brother says. She always has. Maybe someday she will learn. I seriously doubt it! Sissy is actually working toward her MSW which both scares me and makes me very proud.

Living on the Face of the Sun

"Isn't that just kick you in the crotch, spit on your neck
fantastic!"
~Rachel from "Friends"

People flock to Florida in the summertime for
a lovely week of rest and relaxation on the
beach. They love it. It is beautiful. It is balmy. There
is water everywhere. They tan to an exquisite golden
brown in a short time. They eat scrumptious seafood
in quaint little restaurants on the beach. How lucky we,
the natives, are to live here. How wonderful to have
the sun, sand, and sea at our back door. How fantastic
to always have warm weather. BAH HUMBUG! It is
searing in South Florida. It is much as I assume living
on the face of the sun would be.

It is early summer. The temps are already hovering
in the mid to high nineties. The heat index is over a
hundred on most days. That is ridiculous. By August,
it will inevitably be right around 150 degrees. We will
all melt. As it is now, we get up early in the morning to
shower because if we wait too late (any time after six)
we don't have to even turn on the water. It just drips
directly from our pores and pools right down into our
butt crack. This is gross. This is our life, living on the
face of the sun.

After our showers, Sweetie gets ready to go to
work. She does so gladly because it is cold there. She

has to wear long sleeves. From November until April, she drags to work in the morning. She dreads it. She wants to retire. Then around mid-May, she gets a spring to her step in the morning. She tap dances out the door whistling, "High-ho, high-ho, It's off to work I go." This lasts until about the end of October when the foot-dragging begins again.

I, however, work from home. I am not a happy camper. I have continuous boob sweat. I no longer wear underwear. My makeup runs off my face. My hair curls wildly and grows bigger by the minute. The dogs lay around me with their tongues hanging out. They plead with their big brown eyes for me to do something, anything, to cool them off. I take them outside and water them. Yep, in addition to the plants, we have to water the dogs. I turn on the hose and they just stand under the stream and look at me as if I am a goddess. So, I water myself as well. I *am* a goddess. It is wonderful to stand there under the hose with my doggie-children. We have a pool as well. The water feels like bath water. When I get in there, I don't swim. I shave my legs. I am very resourceful. Sweetie just sits on the steps and grumbles about how the pool should be cold just as the house should be. Somehow this takes the fun out of having a pool, at least from May until October.

At about 2:00 PM, the heat really kicks up. That is when I apologize profusely to the doggie-children and head for the door. I jump in the Jeep and make my daily run to the grocery story. Once there, I grab a cart and walk slowly to the frozen food section. I hang out there, sticking my head in each freezer door pretending to peruse which brand of ice cream/frozen vegetable/ waffle/meal-in-a-bag is best. This usually takes about an hour. I then roll up to the checkout, purchase a Diet

Pepsi and head for my next stop, Wally-World. When I arrive, I mingle. I am on a first-name basis with the guys in electronics, the ladies in the craft section, everyone in frozen foods, and most of the cashiers. I see many of the same customers each day as well so I believe that this is quite a common practice for folks that live on the face of the sun. We wave, say "hello," and ask about each other's kids. It is rather like belonging to a social club except that we don't have to pay dues.

Don't think we don't have air conditioning. We do. We also have a $500.00 a month power bill! No joke. Sweetie keeps the A/C set on 68 degrees. It never gets down to that. We have two thermometers to measure how miserable we should be. At this moment, one reads 78 and the other reads 83 so the median temp is 80.5 degrees. Inside. The. House. With three fans running at full force. Yes, I know that having three fans running sounds very redneck. That is okay. I am from Georgia. I am a redneck, albeit a reformed one. Sweetie says she is NOT a redneck but she is loving the fans so I guess that makes her a de facto redneck. We might even put a big ol' fan in the window soon. Redneck heaven. Yee haw! I do not care as long as it cools this house off. 80.5 degrees is at the "nasty miserable" stage, 82 degrees is totally "bitch miserable." We are on our way up. FAST!

Sweetie called three different air conditioning companies yesterday to get them to come out and give us an estimate on a new unit. I heard her tell the guys on the phone that she "wanted the damn vents to rattle out of the wall," and that she would "hunt them down like dogs if it didn't cool correctly." The temp was at 82.5 when she made the calls…as I said, "bitch miserable!" She says that she will "pay ten grand to the first person that can make the air work the way she wants it to."

She is desperate. Living on the face of the sun can be very expensive.

We have shut all of the Big Bertha hurricane shutters on the east and west sides of the house in order to keep out as much sun as possible. We keep all the lights off. It is like living in a cave. It is getting to me. I have started drawing stick figures on the walls. Someday, people will know exactly what we went through just by "reading" the drawings. They will know it was not pleasant. They will know we suffered. They will feel for us. They will see from my art that there is no longer any cuddling in the bed at night. We tried a few times but we stuck together and actually made farting sounds when we forced ourselves apart. You know, the sound that little boys make when they cup their hands under their armpits and flap their arms really hard? Not very sexy, I know. Speaking of sex, not so much. "Bitch miserable" heat truly ruins the mojo. That sucks! I miss it. Not enough to do it and get stuck together, but I think of it sometimes. Well, more than sometimes. But the heat…November is not really so far away or so it seems when it's this hot, I can wait. The drawings will also show that we can no longer cook in the house. Thank heavens for the grill. Did you know that you can actually make spaghetti on the grill? Well, you can. Pancakes are a bit harder but I'm learning. I am documenting everything with my cave drawings. I want people to understand what we went through day by day, living on the face of the sun, aka South Florida.

One night, Sweetie and I were sitting on the sofa watching some goober wiggle his eyebrows on "America's Got Talent" and I heard "OOOOOHH" coming from Sweetie's direction. It was a very loud "OOOOOHH," and it scared me and the doggie-children dreadfully. I jumped and squealed and the dogs threw back their heads and howled. I looked over at Sweetie to see if she had suffered a heart attack or some equally horrific crisis. She was sitting in the yoga "Seated Pose" much like Buddha. Legs crossed, back straight, arms on knees, thumb and middle finger touching in a circle, eyes half closed, face orgasmic, "OOOOOHH," coming from her very core. I was petrified. Sweetie had flipped. She needed help. Badly. Sweetie does not do yoga. I'm the hippy-dippy one. Her poor hot mind had snapped. I grabbed her and shook her.

"What the hell?" I bellowed.

"OOOOOHH, baby, can you feel it? Can you? Reach up. Feel. Oh baby, just feel," she gleefully moaned.

"Huh," I breathed. "You are scaring me. Are you OK? Do you hurt? What is happening?"

"No, I do not hurt. I feel cold air. Did you hear me? COLD. AIR. And it is good, baby. Real good. OOOOHH!"

"Cold air? Where? Give me some…" I demanded with much excitement.

She grabbed me and pulled me over beside her and I'll be damned, I felt it too.

"I feel it," I squealed. "Does this mean I am gonna get laid tonight? We can do it right here. Right where the wonderful cool air is." Hey, I take it when and where I can get it. I might not have to wait until November. A girl's got needs. Like I said, I am resourceful…and horny. Mostly horny.

Sweetie rolled her eyes at me, as she does a lot. She leaned back again and enjoyed the blessed moment of cold air. And that was just about how long it lasted. A moment. Then it went away again. Sweetie slumped into "dejected dog" pose. Maybe she knew more about yoga than I thought. I would have to draw a stick figure of that. I simply pouted when I realized that I was probably going to have to wait until November to get laid. Tears started to roll down both of our faces. They blended with the sweat draining from our pores. The dogs ran over to lick the water off us. They have become resourceful as well. We decided to just go to bed and almost immediately fell into a miserable sleep. On opposite sides of the bed. Not touching. We knew that tomorrow would be just the same.

And it was.

I awoke the following morning at around 7:00 AM and looked at the thermometer. It was already 83.3 degrees. IN. THE. HOUSE. With three fans running and the air conditioner set on 68 degrees. This was way past "bitch miserable." This was "murderous miserable." I blew a kiss to the dogs over my shoulder and sprinted out of that hell hole as fast as possible. I wondered if Wally-World was open yet. Janie was working in frozen foods and she doesn't mind if I just crawl in amongst the frozen veggies and sit for a while as we chat. She has the sweetest kids! One is about to graduate. She is also a great cook and we exchange ideas and coupons as I cool off amongst the peas and corn. Maybe she would give me an idea of something to cook tonight outside. On. The. Grill.

As I pulled into the store parking lot, I breathed a sigh of relief. It was open and there sat Janie's little red Toyota right in front. I threw my car in park right beside her vehicle and ran cheetah-like to the front door. Cool was only a few feet away. I waved my hands above my head and shouted, "Hallelujah!" People stared. I did not care. Seriously, have you seen "The People of Wally-World?" No? Look it up online. There are pictures! I am the blonde in shorty pink pajamas and a pink streak in my hair sitting amongst the frozen peas and corn, right after the picture of the man with the "I Heart Justin" T-shirt and cutoff short-shorts that show a part of his penis. Ain't I cute?

Remember this little story if you ever even think about moving to South Florida. It may make you revisit your decision. It is God-awful hot down here on the face of the sun and you may find yourself never getting laid. Well, at least not during the summer, which is approximately nine months of the year. If you decide to move down here anyway, c'mon over to the Wally-World on Congress. I am there most every day. Come visit me in frozen foods. We'll swap recipes.

Dykes Love Mike

"Nothing takes the taste out of peanut butter quite like
unrequited love."
~Charlie Brown

In response to Sweetie's desperate phone call for
an estimate for a new air conditioner, today the
nice man from E*B*B Air, Jim, showed up. Sweetie met
him at the door with a porcelain bowl of Beluga caviar
on a bed of crushed ice. It was prepared in the Malossol
method which, I found out, means lightly salted. Sweetie
told me that this is preferred by connoisseurs. How the
hell did she know that? We are certainly not caviar
connoisseurs. Pizza connoisseurs definitely...but not
stinking caviar. She served it with a plate of toast points,
lightly browned. For Jim's drinking pleasure, she had
a bottle of Louis Roederer Cristal. I had egg salad and
grape juice for lunch. Not sure this is fair. Just saying.

She had a pair of slippers and a Stradivarius
Churchill cigar for Jim's happiness as well. She wanted
to be sure that he was in a state of complete relaxation
as he went from room to room doing up our little
estimate. I do believe he could have gotten laid if he
played his cards right. She was overwrought and would
probably do just about anything in the name of cold,
frosty comfort.

Jim finished up all of his figuring and sat down
at the dining table to talk about what we needed. She

stood by and fanned him while having me peel grapes and feed them to him. I am not sure how I got pulled into her shenanigans. I suppose that desperate times call for desperate measures. He started talking about SEER and the tonnage. Oh my stars, this excited her to no end. She lit up like Rockefeller Center at Christmas.

"Honey, did you hear that. It is an 18 SEER. Wow! That is phenomenal," she said with exhilaration.

"Ummm hmmm," I replied. "Sure, Sweetie."

"But babe it is a four ton unit. That will rattle the vents. And it's a York," she continued.

"That's nice Sweetie. Just super." I had tuned out by this point. I didn't need specifics. I needed nipple freezing frost.

The nice man from E*B*B asked, "How did you hear about the York brand?"

"From Mike," Sweetie belted out with vigor.

"Mike," he asked questionably.

"Mike Holmes," she told him proudly. "You do know Mike don't you?" She was acting like everyone should know the Mike of which she spoke so reverently.

"Ummm, No, I don't think so," Jim shook his head.

I felt it necessary to chime in here, "Mike Holmes. You know from "Holmes on Homes" on *HGTV*. She never misses an episode. She *loooovvves* him. All dykes love Mike. Didn't you know that?" I was gushing and batting my eyes now. Sweetie was not amused.

"Just hush," she admonished. "I do not love him. I think he is a noble man. He is a true hero. He fixes people's homes the right way. Everyone should do it just like Mike. And, Mike uses York units."

"Oh," Jim murmured a bit uncomfortably. I guess the dyke talk threw him off. So he took a stiff drink of Cristal and ate some more Beluga then continued. "So the unit will be $7,810.00. That includes blah, blah, blah." (At least that is what I heard) "You are eligible for an FPL rebate and an instant rebate and blah, blah, blah." (I had tuned out again) "Your total due at install will be $6,435.00. Then there is a mail-in rebate of $1,000.00 that you will receive as well...blah, blah, blah."

"And, when could you do the installation?" she asked with craving in her voice. I swear this guy actually could have gotten laid with all the need flowing from Sweetie's pore! Ick!

"Wednesday," was his answer.

"I love you," Sweetie whispered pitifully.

"Huh," he said with a strange look on his face.

"Ummm, errrrr, I just said that would be perfect," she stammered, her pink cheeks giving away her embarrassment. "Let's do it."

Jim was excited. He had a full belly, a nice buzz and he had made the sale. "Fantastic."

Sweetie wrapped up the rest of the caviar, the champagne, some grapes, another cigar and the new slippers and sent Jim on his way with a hearty handshake that I had to break apart before she broke his arm. She was just a little spirited and I guess she hoped the gifts would make sure he did the job right and on time.

Just like Mike!

❧❧❧❧

Finally, Wednesday morning arrived and the nice men from E*B*B Air Conditioning were here to install our new four ton York air conditioning system.

It was 7:30 A.M. and I was sitting in the house which already had a temperature of 88 degrees Fahrenheit. I had sweat dripping from every pore. I had armpit sweat, boob sweat, and butt crack sweat. I know sexy right? I was also suffering from "No Air Conditioning in South Florida (NACSoFlo)." NACSoFlo is a regional syndrome that is a bit like Tourette's combined with OCD in that it makes one blurt out a series of random thoughts in the same order over and over. Since the heat started jacking up at an alarming rate that morning, I was spitting out the same few sentences repeatedly. I do believe the sweet little A/C boys were scared. Maybe that would make them work harder and finish faster.

Our conversation began something like this: "Hello, ma'am, could you open the back gate for us so that we can bring your absolutely wonderful new cooling system in and install it?" asked the very tall and very skinny Ryan.

"Juno, if you don't stop barking I will lock you in that bedroom right now," I answered while swinging the gate back. Juno is a very protective Min-Pin. She is extremely loud.

"Ma'am, could you come and look at this so that you will know exactly what I did here," asked Daniel, the shorter and stockier bald installation guy.

"Cricket, do not dare bite that man. He is trying to cool us all off," I replied while glancing at the wires that were hanging from the unit helter-skelter. Cricket, the smaller German Shepherd, is quite the little nipper.

"Could we please get some water?" the boys asked in unison.

"Piper, stop gnawing at that man's leg right this minute!" I screeched as I threw two bottles of water in the general direction of the guys. Piper, our 115 pound German Shepherd, is teething a bit. Legs are her favorite.

"Ma'am we can't put the thermostat where you wanted it because that is a load-bearing wall of concrete. Don't worry though, I will patch up the big ol' hole that I cut out of it," Ryan said.

"If you three don't stop barking at the top of your lungs, I am going to cut out your voice boxes," I told the dogs loudly while waving off Ryan and the hole in the wall. Sometimes the dogs just bark. In tandem. Loudly. I glanced quickly at the holes. They were huge and ragged. There won't be any patching those up without the help of a concrete guy. I was too hot to give a rat's ass.

At about noon the phone rang, "Hi honey. Just checking in. How are you and the dogs making out with no air?" Sweetie queried from her air conditioned office.

"It is 88 degrees in here. My brain is freaking fried. How the hell do you think I feel?" I yelled into the receiver.

"But how is everything looking. They have not made any holes in the wall have they? Are they doing it right? Are they doing it like Mike?" she continued.

"I hate you," I answered. "And I hate Mike."

"Excuse me?" she said.

"Juno, if you don't stop barking I will lock you in that bedroom right now," I hollered. Juno heard her name and walked out of the bedroom panting to see what all the commotion was about. She then turned her stubby little tail up at me and marched right back into the bedroom. I think I heard her curse me. This was not new to her. The air had been out for weeks. She was used to mommy's NACSoFlo. It led to delusions.

"Alrighty, then, I will talk to you later babe," Sweetie said as she hung up hastily.

"Ma'am, we are going to start installing the baffle in just a few minutes," Ryan said.

"Cricket, do not dare bite that man. He is trying to cool us all off," I bellowed while wiping the sweat from underneath my boobs and nodding at Ryan. Cricket licked Ryan's boot as if apologizing for her mommy's behavior.

"Can you come here and let me show you how to use the new thermostat?" inquired Daniel at about 2:30 PM.

"Piper, stop gnawing at that man's leg right this minute," I roared while walking over to Daniel. Piper, who had been sleeping on the sofa, looked up at me quizzically then swiftly fell back asleep.

"We are going to turn on your unit in about an hour or so. If you could start closing the doors and windows and opening up the vents that would be great," Ryan told me seven hours after the work had commenced.

"If you three don't stop barking at the top of your lungs, I am going to cut out your voice boxes," I shrieked as I got up to do as I was told.

"Ummm, ma'am, the dogs are in the back yard. They are not barking. Are you okay?" Ryan inquired with concern.

"It is 88 degrees in here. My brain is freaking fried," I told him while pulling my shirt over my head to try and find a breeze to dry my boobs off. I have no shame.

The phone rang, "Hun, I am just checking in. Make sure they calibrate the air flow in each room so that the pressure..." Sweetie began. This was her

32nd phone call of the day just to "check in."

"I hate you and I hate Mike!" I howled.

"Alrighty then, I have a meeting. Be home soon. I love you." She said as she dropped the phone quickly.

"Ma'am, you are all hooked up. Come here and feel that cold, frosty, arctic air flow," Daniel said just a few minutes later.

I stood in front of a vent. It truly was "rattling out of the wall," as Sweetie had demanded. The air was sumptuous! "I love you," I cried out in pure ecstasy as I kissed Ryan and Daniel's dirty boots. They glanced at me with befuddled expressions then ran for their truck.

It is amazing what good air conditioning can do for a person. I am cured. No more NACSoFlo. I had to admit that Sweetie was right. It had to be done right.

Just like Mike!

꙳ ꙳ ꙳ ꙳

Addendum

Shhhh...If you tell Sweetie this I will swear that I never said it and that you are lying through your blow-hole! But, this time, she was right! We needed the repairs done the way Mike would do them. And, maybe, just MAYBE, I have a teeny, tiny, itty, bitty crush on him too. But I don't wanna sleep with him! He is a big ol' burly dude and not my type even if my type were men...which they aren't. Also, he's kinda baldish and wears overalls and I am not sure about that total package. Maybe if he just had one or two, but all three...? Shit, I am delusional. I don't even know what I am even blathering on about. I have been in the heat too long and my brain is fried. Ignore this paragraph. Oh, I guess it's a bit late for that...well, hell...Have a great day y'all. There, I am ending on a positive note so the paragraph is not a total waste! I'm good like that.

Did you see THE SIZE of that thing?

"I belong, and my penis, it be long."
~Jarod Kintz

Sweetie and I went to Gay Days in Orlando last year. We had tickets to see Michelle Balan and Vickie Shaw. I was stoked. Sweetie, not so much. You see, I am a social butterfly. I must talk to, hug, pat, and swap information with most everyone that I meet. Sweetie loves to go to shows but all of the schmoozing leaves her cold. I figure that's okay though because I can really do some schmoozing. I could be a professional social butterfly. Put me in a crowd and I sprout wings, burst out of my cocoon (or my clothing…but that's another story for another day), and my mouth becomes unhinged. This is when Sweetie steps back and allows me to "act a fool." She shakes her head as her eyes roll back, she mutters a bit, and squeezes the soup out of my hand when I start saying too much. This happens often. Very, very often!

Anyway, we got to the hotel where the Gay Days Expo was being held. I was giddy. This was my first "gay" event being as I had not been "out" very long and I was ready! I hopped out of the truck and headed toward the pool where I could hear all of the thumping music playing. I did not know that there were two pools. There was a male pool and a female pool. Somehow we ended up at the male pool. Oh my goodness. I have never seen so many pee-pees in my life. I have two sons and their friends used to hang out at the house all the time. I have seen pee-pees! I have seen lots of them as little boys don't really care who is around. They will run naked through a grocery store on a dare, tally-whackers swinging. But this was totally different. The first guy that I saw had on a swimsuit, and I use that word very loosely, that was approximately two inches wide and as transparent as a moth's wing. He also had a toy gun in a holster and a cape. Okay. I am open-minded. I can handle this. So, I whacked Sweetie in the arm with my elbow and whispered (kinda loudly), "Did you see that? Did you see the size of that thing?"

"HUSHHHH," she hissed. "Do not say a word. I mean it. Do you hear me? Not one damn word!"

"Yes, Hun. I've got it. I'm okay. I'll be good now," I said sweetly. Then, "OH. MY. GAWD. LOOK. AT. THAT!" I screeched.

Robin, you know from "Batman and Robin," flew right by me. He was followed closely by a beautiful man in a white, fully see-through, string bikini. The man in white was striking. My youngest son, Buddy, is a model so I notice jawlines and this guy had an amazing jawline. He also had a very visible pecker. I mean a totally, completely, utterly discernable penis. His jawline was remarkable. His johnson was not.

"Sweetie," I spoke sort of quietly...I really was trying to keep it down. I was just truly excited. "Look at that. He has a gorgeous jawline but why would he want to show his little ding-a-ling? Both of my boys wee-wees were bigger at birth!"

"OH MY GOD! Will you stop yelling? Everyone in the entire state of fucking Florida can hear you. Do you even know how loud you are?" Sweetie ground out through clenched teeth. I swear that woman is going to get TMJ one day if she doesn't stop all that that jaw clenching. Her getting TMJ would not be a good thing for me. I want her to be able to use her jaws as often and as vigorously as possible. Just saying.

"I am not loud. I was whispering. Kind of. But look at his poor inchworm. It's tiny," I replied. "Why do you think he'd want everyone to see it? I would think that the other guys would point and laugh. They do that in school you know? Why, when I was teaching…"

"For the love of all that is holy, please just shut up! And while you are at it, close your eyes just a bit. You look like the guy in *Young Frankenstein*," she whispered. She is a really good whisperer. I had to lean in to hear her. Maybe I could use some pointers after all.

She then turned on her heels and left me. Right there in the middle of all of the pee-pees. I stayed there and waved and talked and generally got to know a few of the guys. A very sweet bunch they were, even if they did dress a bit ummm, well, risqué. After an hour or so, I headed off to find my love. I didn't have to look far. She was hunkered in a corner behind a plant trying very hard to blend in. It was not working. She must have forgotten to put on sunscreen because she was beet red and that really stood out behind all the greenery.

"Hey Sweetie," I hollered raucously as I ran over. "I made some new friends. Troy is the guy in the white string. He didn't realize how small the suit made his package look until I pointed it out. He went and switched to a dark blue one and it is so much better. See, just look at it. It looks practically bulbous now," I was pointing excitedly as Troy waved back eagerly. "Tim is the guy with the gun and he really got a kick out of me when I asked if that was a gun in his spandex or if he was just happy to see me. HAHA! Pretty funny huh?" Tim drew his toy gun and blew in the end then gave me a cute wink. I just loved my new friends.

Sweetie was grabbing at my arms to keep me from motioning my new chums over. "If you say another word I am going to cut your throat. I swear. I really will this time. I know I have threatened it before, but I mean it at this moment. I will kill you right here and step over your cold, dead body," she muttered.

"Sheesh, you are touchy today aren't you?" I asked as we walked inside toward the expo. "Would you like to borrow some of my meds? They will calm you down in ten minutes flat!" I offered graciously. I always tried to take good care of my woman.

She pulled me directly into a room off to the right which, to my delight, turned out to be the over-eighteen area. Holy moly! I am not innocent. I am an experienced woman. But the things I saw there...

"Sweetie," I bellowed pointing. "Look at the size of that thing. Where would you put that? I've seen horses smaller than that."

That's when I noticed the small pocket knife that Sweetie was fingering slowly. I had not noticed her pull that from her pocket. She is sure stealthy, that one. I glanced up at her and noticed that her eyes were glazed over. I knew then that I was in trouble and we had not even gotten to go to the show yet. I dropped to one knee and kissed her hand. I promised her that I would be good. I assured her that I would take my own meds right that second and that they would calm *me* down. I told her that I loved her. I talked her down. Crisis averted, this time. But there were still a lot of Gay Days to go...and she never even noticed that I had crossed my fingers stealthily behind my back!

Final Destination Part 63 ~ The Death of the Happy Lesbian Housewife

"Pat-downs and seeing through their clothes is one thing, but the PORNO music is a little much." ~politicalhumor.about.com (Daniel Kurtzman)

I recently took a trip to Canada. I was to be gone for two weeks to visit family. Sweetie did not like this planned time away from each other. She pouted a little bit. I wanted to see my kiddos though so I bought the ticket and assured Sweetie that I would be home after just "thirteen sleeps." I woke early on the day of departure and Sweetie and I headed for the airport. As we drew close to the airport, I reminded her which airline I was flying. You see, Sweetie is a "dropper-offer" at airports. She pulls up to the door, grabs your bags, plants a VERY quick kiss on your cheek while whispering, "I love you." She then smacks you on the butt, waves and takes off. The first time this happened, I was surprised, dismayed, and had hurt feelings. The next time I kind of "got it" and even somewhat expected it, but it still hurt a tiny bit. This time, I was prepared for it. There would be no expectations other than the quick grab, kiss, smack, "I love you", wave, and taillights. No hurt feelings either. Well, maybe just a tiny bit of heartache, but I was learning Sweeties little idiosyncrasies. Imagine my surprise when she drove past the drop-off area.

"Sweetie," I said. "You missed the turn for the drop-offs. You will have to go back around."

"I am parking," she announced. "I want to walk you in."

"Huh? Why?" I asked in confusion.

"Because I am going to miss you terribly and I want to walk into the airport and spend every last minute that I can with you." She replied.

"What'd I do?" I asked.

"Nothing, I just want to be with you, honey."

"Did you have a premonition, Sweetie? Am I going to die?" I asked fearfully. "I mean, I know that I am the premonition-haver around here but you know I don't generally have them about myself. Maybe you are seeing something for me. Is it bad? I can take it. Just tell me!"

"No, babe, nothing like that. I just want to be with you for as long as I can. Is that okay with you?"

"You did. You did have a premonition or a dream or something like that. The plane is going down. A bird is going to hit us. I am going to die!" I was getting hysterical.

"No babe. You are not going to die," she reassured me as she parked and jumped out for my luggage. "I just love you. Now let go of the death grip that you have on the dash and let's go."

She grabbed my hand to pull me out and we started walking toward the doorway to my *Final Destination*. You know that movie right? All these students get on a plane and then a kid has a premonition and goes all ape-shit and several pupils run off the plane. The aircraft takes off then blows up and then death comes around to collect the ones that got off. Various sequels were made and now it was my time. I was sure of it!

I was going to die. This was just like the beginning of that movie. Everything was all bass-ackward. What the hell was I going to do? I kept feeling that if I could just make Sweetie do things normally, it would all be okay. God, maybe she was making me OCD. I'd worry about that later, if there was a later. Oh God, what if there was no later? For now, I just needed to stay alive. I needed to get Sweetie OUT. OF. THAT. AIRPORT!

We went hurriedly to the check-in area and I looked up at Sweetie and said "Thank you for coming this far. I got it now. I will call you when I get to Toronto. I love you. Bye now. Be careful on the way home. See ya—" I sounded like an auctioneer.

"Honey," she interrupted. "Slow down. I am going with you as far as they will let me. Don't you get it? I want to be here with you."

"What is wrong with you? Are you sick? Are you dying? Or, did you do something? Are you planning to leave me here never to return to get me? What is going on? Is this your way of getting rid of me?" I was shrieking at this point. Maybe if I caused a scene and embarrassed her, she would get the hell out. Sweetie did not like scenes.

The authorities were starting to look at me now. Crap, I always get the "extra-special" treatment. You know the one. They search every body cavity that you have with a wonderful wand and then feel you up just for shits and giggles. It has to be because I obviously look the part of a terrorist with my blonde hair, blue eyes, ready smile, and southern accent. I am for sure going to get *treated* again today due to the tone of my voice and the panic on my face.

"Babe, calm down. I just want to be with you for as long as I can. That's all. No other reason. I am going to miss you terribly." Then she reached down and kissed me. SHE. KISSED. ME. Right in front of everyone. She does not do that either. A quick peck on the cheek, yes. A full on kiss on the lips, nope, nada, nix, never.

I knew then that she obviously knew something "otherworldly." She had experienced a trance dream just like the Long Island Medium. She knew that I would never be back and she was trying to make it easier. She was saying goodbye in her own way.

"TELL ME." I screeched. "Tell me what the hell is going to happen to me. You ain't fooling me sister. Are there locusts swarms inside the brakes? Did a cat have a litter of kittens in the motor? What is it? Speak!"

"Oh for the love of God," she said. "You told me that you liked to be walked into the airport. It is important to you. I am trying to give you what you need. That's all. I promise."

"Ummm, Hmmm, whatever you say, lie if you want. Do what will help you sleep at night," I thought. But what I said was, "Thank you honey. That is so kind of you."

Time had come to go through security. She *had* to leave me now. "See ya," I chirped in a brightly fake voice while waving like a mad woman. "Thanks for coming with me. I appreciate it and I love you so very much." I was losing it. Would this be the last time that I would see her?

"I will miss you, baby," she said and gathered me in her arms for another loving kiss. "Don't forget to call on your layover. I love you very much."

This was all just bizarre. I turned to look back one last time, expecting my Sweetie to be long gone. She was not. She was still standing there at the gate jumping up and down, waving, and making the "I love you" hand sign to me. She has never, as long as I've known her, made that hand sign to me and I knew then for sure. I was a dead woman. D-E-A-D!

"Oh Lordy," I said aloud to no one in particular. Should I not go? If I didn't, would death just track me down the way it did in the movies? I didn't want to spend my whole life looking around for that big black embalmer guy who worked in the morgue in all the flicks to come after me. His voice alone was scary as hell. "What do I do? I am too young to die. I certainly don't want death to *follow me* the way it did those teenagers. Have mercy…now I have to pee," I was muttering along the way.

Then I heard a loud, gruff, female voice, "You, Blondie. Yea, you. C'mere. You talking to yourself or to someone else?"

It was a security guard. A very cute, very butch, red-haired, dyke with a big ol' wand. She was staring at me as if I was a nutter. I felt like a nutter so no wonder she was glowering at me that way.

"Umm, myself," I stammered blushing a bit.

"Come with me then. We need to check you out a bit more closely," she said.

"Well, alrighty then. What a surprise. Is it the blonde hair? The accent? Lead the way," I told her.

As we walked off together for my "closer check," she looked over her shoulder quickly and whispered, "Actually it is because of the woman you walked up with. Do you know her? The one that is back there skipping around and blowing kisses at you? Is she a danger to you? A stalker maybe?"

I glanced back at my Sweetie. She looked so beautiful. She was trying so hard to give me what I needed. Love filled me. "Oh no," I assured her. "That is the woman who loves me with her whole heart. Am I a lucky lady or what?"

She quirked one eyebrow at me and did not seem at all convinced of Sweetie's sanity as she said, "If you say so. Now, spread'em sweet cheeks and let's see what we find."

And, with a smile on my face and love in my heart, I did just that. I knew that if this was to be my Final Destination, I would take off being adored and that I would leave this earth loved. If this was to be my last day on earth, I would also accept Sergeant Cutie-Pie's Magic Wand happily. I ain't no dummy and I like me a woman with a badge!

Saskatchewan In The Springtime
Or
Skunks and Blizzards and Kerosene, Oh My!

"I chose the road less traveled and now I don't know where the hell I am!"
~A reference to Robert Frost in *The Road Not Taken*

B eing out of town without Sweetie can cause some problems. Sweetie does not like me to be gone from home more than three nights. She pouts a bit. She also knows me. She knows that I love a bit of an adventure. She is not a fan of my adventures. As a matter of fact, she absolutely hates them. I have a tendency to strike out on my own just to explore. She does not like me to go to the store after dark by myself. Well, suffice it to say, one night my son Bubba and I had an adventure of epic proportions. Sweetie will not be amused! Allow me to tell you about my little escapade in Saskatchewan, Canada. Just don't you dare tell Sweetie…deal?

It all began when Bubba and I started out on a business trip to Regina, Saskatchewan one evening at about 6:00 PM. It is a two-hour drive. In good weather. If you can follow directions. If you have a sense of direction. BAM. BAM. BAM. Three strikes. We should have known better and just turned around then. But that would have been too easy, and not nearly as much fun! The trip out there was rather uneventful if you don't count the fact that we headed the wrong way out of town and had to do a cloverleaf to get back on the highway headed in the right direction. The weather was cold but clear. We made fairly good time, met with our client, and got ready to head back when Bubba decided that he would like to run by The Coffee Shoppe for a hot coffee and a muffin. This is when things began to get weird.

We headed toward the edge of town and saw the flashing Coffee Shoppe sign with a drive-thru, pulled in, and got our order to go. Fortified with a strong coffee and a delicious chocolate muffin, we pulled back onto the road. Then, something strange happened. When we pulled back on the road headed out of town, we ran smack up on a skinny little pole that had not been there just minutes ago. There were several of them right in the middle of the road. POLES. WITH. NO. LIGHTS. It was after nine and very, very dark. Who the hell in their right mind runs out and sticks little poles in the road in the dark? Anyway, we almost cut the car in half before we got past the poles with no purpose. After cursing very loudly and trying to make sure that we had not peed our pants, or worse, we headed on out of town. We did not know that the poles were the entrance to some type of vortex and we had just entered a twilight zone. From here on out it will be known as the TZ for brevity!

Within minutes of entering the TZ, we noticed that it had begun to spit snow. Oh, how lovely. A bit of snow for our ride home. Fun! We turned up k.d. lang's "Halleluiah" and sang lustily along. Then came the lightening and rain…just fifteen minutes away from the cute little snow spits.

"What the hell?" asked my son.

"I don't know. You live here not me. Is this normal?" I replied.

Then it just stopped. No precipitation whatsoever. We breathed a sigh of relief and sang along with Miley Cyrus as she made "The Climb." Our good fortune lasted for about another fifteen minutes as we worked our way through songs by Nickelback and Kid Rock, then BAM! Snow hit us hard. We could barely see the road for the flakes that were the size of golf balls.

"Don't you people have weather warnings up here?" I asked. "If we were going to have weather like this, they would break in on every single station and alert the entire US of freaking A!"

"Well, no, not unless it is going to be bad…"

"BAD?" I screamed. "I can't see the road! That is hell-a BAD!"

He guffawed.

I glared.

We were crawling along at that point and our trip was stretching interminably. I was beginning to doubt that I would ever see Sweetie again. Did I mention that I only had a light khaki jacket? And, that I wore short sleeves and ballet flats with no socks. I am from South Florida. I don't do cold, freezing, snow. GAH!

Again, just as suddenly as it had all started, it stopped. I told you, TZ vortex! We were picking up speed again and making up some lost time when we saw a big double tanker ahead of us with flashing yellow lights.

"What the hell is that?" Buddy said.

"I don't know…ummm…flashing lights?" I piped up cuz I'm smart like that. You just can't fool me.

There seemed to be smoke coming out the top

of the truck and it was warbling from side to side in a funny manner, so we decided to pass it quickly. As we went by it, we noticed that it was not smoke coming out of it at all. It was liquid. Not good. Really, really not good. The liquid sprayed our tiny little car with a mist and we were suddenly enveloped in the smell of kerosene. GREAT! Our car was covered in KEROSENE. How lovely. We started to giggle. This was not really happening. It just could not be…we were having the same dream. Surely that was what it was.

Then, it really came down. Snow. Big ol' honkin' white flakes flying at us with a force that I had never felt before. Have you ever *felt* snow from inside a car? I had not. The winds started whipping us around on the road. Blowing us to and fro. All I could think to say was, "Well, at least the snow will wash off the kerosene and if some idiot flicks a cigarette out the window, we won't go up in flames!"

My dear, sweet first born looked at me like I had two heads and replied, "There is not really a chance that anyone will flick out anything due to the fact that we seem to be the only car on the damn road except for a wonky kerosene truck that is spraying everywhere. There are not even houses on this road/ Have you noticed…huh? Have you? We are the only ones out here. We are all alone in this holy hell whiteout…do you get it Mother?"

"Well, don't get hysterical, geesh," I said. "You really need to meditate more."

"GAH, I don't meditate, Mother! You do. You are the hippy-dippy one For God's sake!" Bubba yelped. I do not know why my kids call me mother when they get frustrated.

"Well you should for heaven's sake. You are about

to bust a blood vessel—"

"Just shhhhhhh…" he interrupted.

At that moment, I spotted a sign on the side of the road with a moose on it. FUN! "Hey," I said. "Do you think we might see a moose? How fun would that be?"

"We can't even see the road. How would we see a moose unless we hit it? Then we would not have a vehicle because moose are huge. Do you hear me? HUGE! Really big, mean, ugly, freaky animals that would break this tiny little car in half," he yelled.

"But it would be really cool to see one." I pouted.

Once more, the snow stopped and within ten miles lightning started. Kanye West started rapping about gold-diggers and we joined in. The wind picked up and made us feel as if we were on the Tilt-A-Whirl. We thought the worst of it was over. We should stop thinking! It was as if Rod Serling himself opened the heavens of the TZ vortex which we were caught in and dumped a huge bucket of snow right on the highway in front of us, covering everything in sight. We both squealed.

"Can you see the road?" Bubba implored.

"Not very well, but enough to know that we are not on it!" I answered.

"Oh My Good Lord, this is just not right! Not even for Saskatchewan. This is too weird."

"Well, what should—" I started.

BUMP…SWOOSH…

"OH LORD, what did I just hit?" Bubba bellowed.

"A moose," I said excitedly as I was rolling down my window to look. "Oh, no, not a moose. Definitely not a moose. You hit a skunk!"

Stench filled the car, Bubba and I now smelled of a mixture of sweat, kerosene and skunk. Eau de Keroskunk!

This time the snow did not let up. It came all the way home with us, which took over three hours. We reached home at about 1:00 AM, got out of the car, and kissed the soggy, wet, ground and thanked the heavens for allowing us to escape the TZ vortex from Saskatchewan Hell. Then we went in and did the only thing we could think to do: we fell to the floor in a fit of giggles that lasted for a good half hour and had us both rushing to the bathroom several times to keep from peeing our pants.

What an adventure! I love adventures. Sweetie ain't gonna be happy about this though. Not happy at all. I told her that I would be good. I tried. Really I did. Maybe she will never find out about this. One can hope.

❧ ❧ ❧ ❧

The text message said simply, "Tell me some of that was B.S."

The text was from Sweetie and came in fairly quickly after I wrote the: *Saskatchewan in the Springtime Or Skunks and Blizzards and Kerosene, Oh My!* first draft a few days later and sent it for her perusal. She was a bit testy. I could tell by the tone of the text. Some people can't hear tones in texts, but I can. Hers was not nice. I thought it would be better to call her because she was at work. She couldn't get too angry with me there. There were too many people around. HA…good idea! I picked up the phone and slowly dialed her work number. The phone rang, she answered, and I chirped brightly, "Hi Sweetie. How are you?"

Silence.

Uh-oh.

"So, are you having a good day at work, babe?" I asked.

Not a word.

"Hello?" I squeaked.

"Just tell me you made some of it up," she finally said.

"Nope," I said brightly. "I even left some out. I didn't tell about the kerosene eating through the wiper blades so that there was a film and streaks on the window at all times or about the off ramp that was barricaded so that we had to go around said barricades because we didn't know any other way to get where we needed to go or that I talked Bubba into a moose hunt the next night but those suckers are fast so we didn't get one—"

"STOP," she growled through what I assumed were gritted teeth. "Not one more fucking word…"

"But don't you wanna hear about the time we almost went in the ditch and there were these cows…" Sometimes I just don't know when to shut my mouth.

"I am calling the airlines. I am getting you home and then having you put on the "Do Not Fly" list. You can't be trusted to stay out of trouble. Geeze! What were you thinking? Never mind, you weren't thinking. You never think before you act." She said. Then I heard it. There was a click. She had hung up on me. The nerve!

Sheesh, some people just have no sense of adventure! I hope she doesn't mind that I have some people coming over tonight for a nice little séance. That should be a hoot!

Spoiled, The Whole Lot of Them

"Perhaps all artists were, in a sense, housewives: tenders
of the earth household."
~Erica Jong

I have come to the conclusion that Sweetie is
spoiled. I reached this conclusion upon my
return from Canada. When I left, there were plenty of
groceries and Sweetie and the dogs and cat were fed.
When I returned, not so much. Sweetie had greeted me
upon my arrival at the airport with a huge bear hug,
grabbed my suitcases, and then promptly threw me in
the truck. What a sweet welcome. She truly did miss me.

When we got home the dogs greeted me at the
door with expressions that said, "Where were you dear
mommy? We have missed you, we love you, and we are
hungry! Momma is not here with us during the day as
you are so we did not get the proper amount of chicken
treats. We are dwindling to a skeleton-like state. Just
look at us."

Mind you, the dogs are definitely in no danger of
shrinking away. They are just spoiled too. They know
that I am the soft touch that puts chicken in their
bellies for any cute little trick or look they may bestow
upon me. I went to get said chicken treats immediately
because I did not want any of the little ones to fall over
from lack of food and found that there were none.
Sweetie had not gone to the store for Smart Pets! My

poor sweet babies…

I then opened the fridge and noticed that there was no food in there either aside from two apples, an onion, some minced garlic, and condiments out the wazoo. Sweetie was following me around from room to room because she had missed me so much, or so I thought. She looked at me when I opened the refrigerator door and said, "What's for dinner?" Aha, she missed my cooking.

"Well, Sweetie, we can have fried apples and onions with garlic or we can go get groceries," I replied.

"Groceries," she mumbled as if it were a novel idea. "Yes, groceries are good."

So off to the grocery store we went. I bought all the staples as well as some things that just looked good. Sweetie followed along behind me with a glazed look on her face. She was looking at the food as if she were hypnotized. She said the names of everything that caught her eye aloud as if it were a mantra.

"Cheese." "Butter." "Milk." She chanted.

"Cantaloupe." "Chicken." "Peas." People were starting to stare.

"Cake." " Ice Cream." She was beginning to drool.

"Sweetie," I said gently so as not to scare and confuse her. "I have everything we need. Let's go get the animals some food now and then we can head home and I'll cook dinner. okay?"

"Dinner," she said vacantly with a strange half-smile on her face. I must admit Linda Kay Silva's zombie book, *Man Eaters*, entered my mind. A girl never knows when her woman may become a zombie and eat her face off. I seriously wondered if the apocalypse had taken place and she had been bitten and just had not "turned" yet.

(Note to self: Check Sweetie for bites when we get home!)

I checked out and paid as Sweetie stared at each item that went down the conveyor, still repeating their names loudly, her head going back and forth like a dog watching a squirrel on a fence. We then went to the pet store and got chicken treats and food and headed on our way. I was praying Sweetie would not "turn" since I didn't have anything on me to shoot her with.

Once home, I put up the food, fed the dogs and, much to their delight, gave them a chicken treat. I then began to prepare homemade Salisbury steaks with mushroom gravy, mashed potatoes, and mixed white and yellow corn. Sweetie stood at the kitchen doorway with her jaw slack, a bit of drool hanging from the lower corner, eyes glued on the food simmering away on the stove. Poor thing; I now knew that she was either "turning" or in pure bliss over the food. I grabbed a butcher knife. One can't be too careful during a zombie apocalypse.

"Sit Sweetie," I said when dinner was finished. "We can eat now."

I sat her plate in front of her and went back to grab mine so that we could dine together after two weeks apart. When I turned back into the dining room, her food was GONE! I had been away from the table for 57 seconds and every bite of the food had disappeared. Every. Single. Bite. Her plate was clean.

"Sweetie," I said slowly. "Where did your food go? Did the dogs grab it from you? What happened?" I reached under the cabinet and grabbed her crossbow.

"Ate it," she mumbled. "All gone gone. Yummy, yummy in my tummy."

She was starting to scare me a bit. It had to be the

zombies. They ate fast.

What was I to do? Should I go ahead and stab her through the eye? Use the crossbow? Shake her?

"Honey, you mean you ate everything that I put on your plate? In less than a minute, you finished it?" I said as I went with option three and shook the bejesus outta her. She shook her head, looked at me with eyes that were now clear and replied in her normal strong voice, "Hell yeah, and it was a lot better than peanut butter and jelly!" Doesn't she say the sweetest things? She then grabbed me up in a bear hug and said, "Never leave me for two weeks again, honey. I love you and I need you."

Thank God! I thought. *She just loves and misses me and my cooking. Mostly my cooking...*

They are spoiled I tell you. The whole rotten lot of them. But, I can live with that. They are my family after all. I am just glad it was not the beginning of the zombie apocalypse and I can put the crossbow away now. I sure was dreading having to put Sweetie down...

He Should Have Just Bought Her Flowers

"It takes someone really brave to be a mother, someone strong to raise a child, and someone special to love someone more than herself."

~Ritu Ghatourey

Adoration surrounds me from every angle. My breath is coming in short bursts. My heart feels ready to explode. Tears run down my face. Sweetie dabs at them and says sweetly, "Oh honey, why are you crying?"

"This is just so pleasurable, so gratifying and so very sweet. I am just so blissful. I am loved," I reply excitedly. My breath quickens as the end approaches.

"Yes, honey, you are loved very much," she says as she strokes my face tenderly while staring deeply into my eyes with her baby blues. "Always remember this moment. How you feel. Why you feel this way." She reaches down and kisses me satisfyingly, her tongue seeking mine pleasurably.

As I finish, I let out a slight yelp. Love engulfs me yet again. I am falling, falling. My heart throbs. I am in love all over again. Just as I fell in love with him over 20 years ago. On the day he was born. My sweet redhead. My loving, youngest son who is so much like me. Today, on the day that belongs to mothers everywhere, he wrote me a poem. How thoughtful is that? What else were you thinking? Seriously, get your mind out of the gutter! This is not that kind of story.

I had sat down at my computer to work. When I opened my email, there in my inbox was this wonderful slip of prose that Buddy had composed just for me. His first love. His momma.

I was euphoric. He writes, just like me. How wonderful. I felt overwhelming joy and knew that I had to share this with everyone. His words speak the truth. They are stunningly exquisite. His talent is unparalleled.

The first two lines set the tone for the whole poem. The feelings of love and adoration that simply dripped from each syllable overwhelmed me. Grab some tissues. You will need them, as did I.

<u>Ode to Mom</u>
You've taken care of me since the day I was born
You told me it was ok when my poop had corn.
Oh, my gosh. How breathtaking. Can you feel it? Affection permeates each word.
I used to get a lot of stitches in my head
You couldn't see the blood because my hair was red.
"Memories, light the corners of my mind. Misty watercolor memories of the way we were." Barbra said it best.
To me you are like the sun, the moon and the stars
You have always supported me even if I wanted to go to Mars.
I gave him wings to fly. He appreciates this. The tears begin yet again. His iambic pentameter is perfection.

I haven't seen you in a while and I sure miss you a lot

When we die we will surely share a funeral plot.

He lives in California. So far away, and, he misses me. He wants to be linked with me for eternity. Oh, what a remarkable son. **SOBS**

In my heart you will always stay

And I want you to know that I love you on this happy, happy mother's day.

Sob...sob...sniffle...gulp!

~~~~~~

Addendum

This is Sweetie writing. I felt it necessary to step in a finish this for my love. She is in a weeping ball of mush underneath the table. I really don't get all this sappy stuff and am not sure if she is crying from happiness or lamenting over the flow of the...ahem... "poem" that Buddy wrote. He should have just bought her flowers. He is twenty-four years old for Pete's sake! But, what the hell, he made her happy and in the end I guess that's all that matters.

Diversity
A Totally True Text Message

Buddy: Mom, Did you realize that we have almost every ethnic group there is covered in our immediate family?

Me: Nope, Son, I hadn't really thought about it.

Buddy: Well, think about it! You and Sweetie are married lesbians, dad is in a married heterosexual relationship, Bubba is gay and his boyfriend is from another country...

Me: Yeah, I see where you are going here. We are quite a diverse bunch.

Buddy: Hells yeah! Sissy is in an interfaith marriage and I am in an interracial dating relationship... We freaking rock :)

Me: You are right son, pretty cool.

Buddy: You know that I always wanted a black grandma, right? Well, I kinda have one now...

Me: Yes, son, I know. Ever since you were a little boy you talked about that. Other little boys talked about Thomas the Train and you talked about wanting a nice black grandma that would cook for you. Come to think about it, you were a strange little kid. LOL

Buddy: What do you think folks back home would think about us as a family now?

Me: That we were going to hell in a handbasket! You KNOW this would not be accepted back home... your daddy would be the only one...and even he would be questioned in some circles because he is divorced and remarried. But he would be the closest to "normal." The rest of us would be flogged.

Buddy: Ya really think so?

Me: Well, you may be ok. There are more interracial couples there now than when we lived there. And, Sissy may be ok as long as they didn't discuss their religious orientation too much...or not at all. But, me and Bubba, nah, we'd be ostracized or worse!

Buddy: Huh?

Me: It means to exclude or banish a person or persons from a particular group or society, get our asses kicked or get drawn and quartered at noon in the Town Square.

Buddy: Dafuq...Momma you really think so? Is there even a Town Square in our home town?

Me: Yep, there is a Town Square...and it would probably be worse for Bubba than for me and Sweetie because of the "good ol' boys," but yeah I think so.

Buddy: Well, that sucks!

Me: Yeah, Buddy, it does.

Buddy: Well screw them! I seriously think that we have the coolest family in the whole world. Everybody should have a family like ours. We are a colorful jumble of differences and that makes us interesting and beautiful.

Me: I totally agree son.

Buddy: I love you momma.

Me: Love you too, son

Buddy: Can I borrow $50.00?

Me: Go ask your Black Grandma!

The Perfect Kid

"I don't care if you're black, white, straight, bisexual,
gay, lesbian, short, tall, fat, skinny, rich or poor. If you're
nice to me, I'll be nice to you. Simple as that."
~Eminem

I'll never forget his sweet voice saying, "Momma,
I need to tell you something."

His voice was tortured like he had done something
wrong. I smiled though because this was my first born,
my easy child. I just knew that whatever he had to say
wouldn't be "Oh, God Momma I did…" or "Momma,
I didn't mean to but what am I going to do about…?"
Not this kid!

Bubba was, and had always been, my fairly
effortless youngster. His teachers loved him. The other
parents loved him. He was handsome, quiet and polite.
He was also very smart and in the gifted program
at school. A parent's dream, really. The only small
problem that he ever seemed to have was fitting in with
the other kids. I noticed this as early as first grade. I
didn't worry though, not really. Socialization would
come with time. I was sure of it.

By the fourth grade, bullying began and once
Bubba even had to fight physically to defend himself.
At that point, I was not so sure of him being able to
fit in. He tried so very hard but it just never seemed
to work for him. My heart broke for him. I became

involved with the teachers, the administrators as well
as the parents of the bullies. Nothing seemed to work.
So Bubba and I worked together so that he knew how
to avoid situations that would put him in harm's way.
He still did not "fit in" but he was not in danger. As
a mother this hurt but he was still, for all intents and
purposes, the "perfect kid" that I had always known
and I loved him dearly.

Things continued on this course until sixth grade.
He finally found a couple of best friends and a "group."
I breathed a huge sigh of relief. My son was accepted.
My easy child that I held so dear was happy…or was he?
Was I seeing what I wanted to see? Was he pretending?
Did he just want friends so damned badly that he
was willing to settle? Was I worrying over nothing?
I decided to let it go and to let him make his own
decisions. He was smart, brilliant really. He should
know if these people were real friends…shouldn't he?

Fast forward ten years. Bubba had met a girl.
He thought he was in love. I, however, was not so
sure. She was ten years older. She also lived in another
country and had a child. Bubba had always wanted to
move away from our hometown due to bad childhood
memories. He had also always wanted to have children.
So I questioned his motives when he told me that he
was going to marry her and move to her country.
I was devastated. This was my baby. But, this was
NOT my life. I gave my blessing, albeit reluctantly,
and he married her and moved over three thousand
miles away. They immediately started having children
which made me happy. I love my grandchildren! Still,
I worried for HIM. Was HE happy? Was this what HE
wanted? He was so very far away. I could not just hop
in the car and look into his eyes to see if he was telling

me the truth. I needed him to be happy and I felt the only thing that made him that way was his children.

Fast forward ten more years to a not so very pleasant divorce. My heart was aching for my "easy child." In my eyes, he was in a foreign country all alone. He needed to stay there for his children. And, to be honest, he had come to love his new home. He had a great new group of friends, a good job, a social life, and a great new group of friends (did I say that already…A GROUP OF FRIENDS…YAY!).

Then the call came. "Momma, I need to tell you something."

"Okay, Son, what's up?"

"Well…uh…Ummm…err…I don't know how to say this…" he stammered.

"Just say it Bubba. I love you. Nothing will change that." I replied, feeling for the first time that something may be really wrong.

"Damn, I don't know why it is this hard. I didn't think it would be. I called you first for that reason."

I suddenly grinned like a Cheshire cat. I finally realized what he was going to tell me. My heart swelled. Bubba was finally going to be honest. Not with me. With himself! "Go ahead, Son. Tell me what you need to." This was his story, not mine. I would not say it for him. He needed to be the one to tell it.

"Well, Mom, it's just that I'm uh…well…I…" He trailed off.

"Son," I prompted knowing what was coming as I had known since my sweet, easy, loving, smart boy was eight years old. "Just tell me. I will love you forever no matter what!"

"I'm gay Momma," he spat out like I was going to immediately transport to his country, slap him then promptly disown him.

"Oh baby, I am so proud of you! It sure took you long enough to accept yourself for what and who you are. I am proud of your bravery in coming out and choosing to live your life your way. To choose what others may view as the 'hard' way when you had the 'easy' way before when you were married. But, mostly I am proud that you chose to find love. Real love. The kind of love that you have dreamed of."

"So you are not mad at me?" He implored.

"Are you kidding? Son, I am in love with a woman or did you forget that little fact? Why would I be angry with you? I couldn't be prouder of you...not because you are gay but because you are finally being you!" I replied.

"Oh, thank God! I thought that you would think that I was broke or not perfect or..." he prattled.

"Hush, Bubba, you are not broken! You are still my perfect baby boy and I couldn't be prouder of you. I just have one question for you though," I grinned impishly.

"Sure. What, Mom?" He asked

"Are you a top or a bottom?" I asked with my eyes gleaming mischievously.

"OH. MY. GOD. MOTHER!" He yelped just as I heard the click that disconnected us.

Some people are just so sensitive!

Our Home Is In A Perpetual State Of Remodel

"They always say time changes things, but you actually have to change them yourself."
~ Andy Warhol, The Philosophy of Andy Warhol

Last night Sweetie and I ate dinner at the dinner table. It was a banner day. We have not been able to eat at the table for a very long time. You see, our house is in a perpetual state of remodel. At any given time there are screws, hammers, various power tools and/or paint on the table. This makes it extremely hard to eat there without finding metal or paint chips in your mashed potatoes. Let me tell you, mashed potatoes with green paint in them are a bit unpleasant to the eye as well as the palate. Chicken doesn't look really appetizing with nail heads sticking out the top either. Not to mention the dental bills would be astronomical from chewing them. Sweetie has the best of intentions. When she starts a project, she means to finish it in a timely manner. She just tends to find another task to start before the prior one is finished.

We painted the living room about three months ago. Sweetie's job was cutting in the trim. We worked until about 2:00 AM and she still lacked a bit to finish when we went to bed. The next morning dawned and instead of cutting in paint, she cut the upstairs hall carpet out. Our cat, Max, had decided to pee on it for some reason so it smelled slightly. The cutting in of paint was forgotten and up came the hall carpet. We had no carpet to replace it. We also had no flooring. We just had a big hole where the carpet used to be and one wall with a big white stripe at the top of it. Sweetie went out to find flooring and as luck would have it, they do not make our laminate flooring any longer. Oh yay. However, Sweetie did find new cheater blocks to replace the ones that the dogs had chewed. So that is what she brought home. She laid them on the table and that is where they stayed for approximately four weeks along with the hammer and nails to attach them to the walls.

Sweetie had decided that instead of attaching the cheater blocks, she needed to do the doors in the office. She was actually going to replace all the doors in the house but that would come in time. Maybe. She had bought the doors a year before and they had been sitting on the floor of the guestroom. The hardware to attach them was on the (you guessed it, you brainiacs you) kitchen table. She finished one of the doors and came down to fiddle with the cheater blocks. She attached several to the wall without painting them. And, again, you guessed it, the paint made its way to the dining room table. We now had a big hole where the carpet used to be and one wall with a big white stripe at the top of it, one door put up in the office (it needed two) and unpainted cheater blocks scattered around.

I went to California right around this time. When I returned, just a few short days later, there were five boxes of laminate flooring sitting in the middle of the living room. She had been on a search. It paid off. She found some flooring. The receipt was on the dining table. We could no longer eat there. It was too cluttered for even a bird to land…if we had birds in our house…

which we don't. Anyway, we moved to eating off the ottoman in the living room while sitting on the couch. We also got hooked on "America's Funniest Home Videos."

Eating off the ottoman was not the best idea that we had. We have to lean forward and hold our hand under our forks so that the food does not fall on us, the dogs, or the floor. This does not always work however so Sweetie has stains right between the boob area on several of her gray T-shirts. No big deal though as she has 49 of basically the same shirt. I don't have stains because the little dog sits underneath me and catches everything that falls. Something had to give. So, I cleaned off the table. It took about two weeks, but I did it. We still have a big hole where the carpet used to be and one wall with a big white strip at the top of it, laminate flooring lying in its boxes, and unpainted cheater blocks scattered around. But, last night we bought flowers, we turned the lights low, and talked as we actually ate off of the dining room table. It was nice. I wondered how long it would last.

I did not have to wonder long. Sweetie came in a few minutes ago and asked if I thought we should redo the guestroom since my youngest son is coming for a visit in a few weeks. She had several bags from Home Depot in her hands. They went right on the dining room table. Sweetie means well. She means to finish things in a timely manner. She just tends to find another task to start before the prior one is finished.

Anyone for steak and baked potatoes for dinner? It will be served on the ottoman at approximately 7:00 p.m.

Top or Bottom
A Totally True Text Message

Sissy: Mom, Bubba is being mean to me again.
Me: What did he do this time?
Sissy: He sent me a text message…
Me: And, what did you do?
Sissy: Nothing…
Me: Umm hmmm…send me the message!
Sissy: OK but you'll see!

FORWARDED MESSAGE FROM SISSY:

Sissy: So, Bubba, how do you decide who is the top and who is the bottom if you are in a relationship?
Bubba: None of your business
Sissy: But, seriously, I'm curious and so are Buddy and Mom and Sweetie. We wanna know!
Bubba: No they don't. You are the nosy one. YOU want to know.
Sissy: Well, maybeee…
Bubba: What does it matter to you?
Sissy: I don't know. Just curious I guess.
Bubba: Curiosity killed the damn cat…
Sissy: C'mon…
Bubba: Ok. Well, it goes like this. I have this glow-in-the-dark body paint, right? And when things get really going we paint our penises and the…
Sissy: OK, stop! I didn't think you'd really tell me!

Bubba: Well, why'd you ask then?

Sissy: For shits and giggles...

Bubba: Really, you asked ME just for shits and giggles...MWHAHAHA! Next, we have a sword fight...

Sissy: STOP IT! LA, LA, LA DEE DA

Bubba: Nope, you asked...As I was saying, we have a sword fight with our paint-coated penises and it is an epic battle to the dea—

Sissy: Seriously...I hate you right now!

Bubba: battle to the death. It's almost like *Transformers* but with penises instead of cars and the loser is the bottom! My Penis name is Penis-Optimus and I would hope that my partner's would be Mega-Rod. Get it? There, now you have an answer! Happy?

Sissy: I'm telling Mom!

Bubba: You are 30 years old. And I live over 3000 miles away. What is she gonna do?

Sissy: I don't know...ground you or something.

Bubba: You shouldn't have asked.

Sissy: I'm still telling...

Bubba: Whatever!

END OF FORWARDED MESSAGE

Sissy: See Mom, he was mean to me.

Me: Well, you asked!

Sissy: But I didn't think he'd tell me!

Me: Do you KNOW your brother?

Sissy: Well, yeah, but...

Me: Alright then.

Sissy: Whattya gonna do to him?

Me: He is a grown-ass man. I'm doing nothing if he wants to sword fight with his penis. Boys will be boys!

Sissy: MOM! GROSS! Still, he was mean and embarrassed me.

Me: That was your fault. Hey, while we are on the subject of sex, have you ever tried vajazzling?

Sissy: OMG! I gotta go Mom!

Me: :)

STOP TOUCHING ME!

"To win by strategy is no less the role of a general than
to win by arms."
~Julius Caesar

Sweetie and I have a wonderful game that we
play sometimes. It is a game much like the
old, "She's touching me..." "I'm not touching you,"
game that you probably played as a child with a sibling
or close friend. You remember that game? Wasn't it *a
freaking blast*?

Yes, well, the game that Sweetie and I play is just
as much entertaining! This game is called, "Where do
you wanna go?" "No, where do *YOU* wanna go?" There
are several variations on this game. They include, but
are not limited to, "What do you wanna do?" "No, what
do *YOU* wanna do?" or "Where would you like to eat?",
"But Sweetie, I wanna know where *YOU* would like to
eat?" You can play this wonderful game separately or
combine several of the variations to make it even more
exciting.

This weekend was one of the weekends that
Sweetie and I decided, albeit separately, that playing
this game would be of great benefit to our relationship.
So, we played...and played ...and played! The weekend
started off as most weekends do: we woke up and
snuggled a bit and then the games began.

"So, honey, what would you like to do today?"

Sweetie asked.

"I am not sure, Sweetie. What would *you* like to do?" I replied.

"Well, I *need* to mow and clean up the back yard, but then I am open. Unless, of course, you want to do something before that. If so, I can change my plans to make you happy. That is my job after all. So, tell me, what would you like to do?"

"Sweetie, I do not care. You go ahead and mow then we will see what time it is and we can decide what to do after that. How does that sound?" I prodded.

"But we can go ahead and make some plans, right? So, is there anywhere you would like to go?" She switched things up and threw in a different variation. She is very good at this game!

"Not really," I shot back. "Where would *you* like to go?"

"Well, honey, you have been in the house all week. So it is important to me that we go somewhere that you would like to go. So, where might that be?"

"I would like to go wherever *you* would like to go," I thought this was a great move.

"Oh, honey, you can't use that move here. Just tell me where you would like to go and I will take you." I told you that she is good at this.

I thought about this. What would drive her to the brink? What did she hate? *SHOPPING*! Winner, winner, chicken dinner! "Hmm, how about shopping? Would you like to go shopping?"

"Ahhh, babe, shopping? Really?" Sweetie is not much of a shopper. As a matter of fact, she had rather pull her eyelashes out one by one. With her fingernails. Slowly.

"Well, I know that since we have been on Weight

Watchers and have both lost weight, you need a new shirt for work so we could get that!"

"OK, shopping it is. When would you like to leave?" She switched it up again. What the hell? *Point Sweetie!*

"It doesn't matter to me. When would *you* like to leave?" I queried.

"Whenever you want," Sweetie announced with verve.

With growing impatience I said, "Oh no Sweetie, this is your decision since you need to mow the yard. So, when would *you* like to leave?"

"Well, we can leave when I finish mowi—" Sweetie started.

"That's fine Sweetie," I interjected quickly. "But what shall I wear?" Go meee…it's my birthday…go, go, go meee…*I* switched it up this time! *Point Me!*

"Whatever makes you feel good. What would *you* like to wear babe?" Sweetie shot back swiftly.

"I would like to look nice for you. So I would like to know what you would like for me to wear," I told her.

She looked at me with a gleam in her eye, "You always look wonderful to me. Please, honey, wear whatever *you* would like."

"How about my pink and green T-shirt and purple shorts?" I purposefully picked mismatched clothing in order to throw her a curve. "Do you like that that?"

"As I said before, you look wonderful in anything you wear. So, yes, that is fine! You will look smashing no matter what you have on." *Point Sweetie!* She was unflappable. She must have been practicing.

(Note to self: Practice the "What would you like to do/wear/see/eat/etc." game!)

Sweetie headed out to mow and I ran screaming

to the bedroom where I hid my head under the covers. I was trying to figure out how to beat her in this game. I am very competitive and hate to lose at anything. We had been at this for about two hours and nothing had been really decided except that we *were* going to look for her a shirt and I now *had* to wear my pink and green T-shirt and purple shorts. Damn it all, I was going to look like a fool. Or, a clown. Take your pick. But, I would not back down so I got dressed. I added a yellow necklace, blue earrings and orange flip-flops. In for a penny, in for a pound I figured.

When Sweetie had finished the yard, she walked upstairs and said, "Okay, babe, I will jump in the shower then we can go. Oh, and you look...Ummm...very... err...colorful."

"Thank you," I said sarcastically. "I have been thinking. How about we go to the movies?"

Sweetie put her game face on and said, "What movie would you like to see?"

"Oh, my sweet girl, I want to see whatever *you* want to see!" I shot back triumphantly.

"But I thought we were going to go shopping for a shirt," she pointed out.

"But wouldn't you rather go see a movie?" I inquired.

"Would you rather see a movie?"

"I would rather do what *you* want to do," I looked at her innocently. *Point Me!*

"We will go shopping and then we will decide about the movie after," Sweetie growled.

Sweetie finished getting ready to go and we walked to the truck. Our mood was that of two momma lions protecting their pride. We jumped into the truck and headed out.

I looked over at my dear Sweetie and said, "When we find your shirt, I would love to grab a bite to eat before we decide on the movie that we will be watching."

"Great she said. That sounds good…"

I poked Sweetie quite hard on her arm and said triumphantly, "So, Sweetie, what would *you* like to eat?"

"***STOP TOUCHING ME!***" she screeched loudly.

GAME, SET, MATCH, ME!

෴෴

Addendum

Sweetie asked me to add the caveat that I do not always win. I just got to choose this story because I am the writer. If she wants to be the winner, maybe she should write her own damn book!

The Alligator Upstairs

My own heroes are the dreamers, those men and women who tried to make the world a better place than when they found it, whether in small ways or great ones. Some succeeded, some failed, most had mixed results...but it is the effort that's heroic, as I see it. Win or lose, I admire those who fight the good fight."
~ George R.R. Martin

One rainy Sunday afternoon, I was snuggled under my comfy furry blanket watching one of my favorite television shows on the DVR: *Project Runway*. Do not laugh at me. One can learn a lot from this show such as how to make leather biker vests, hem denim, and put together a perfect flannel apron. These are all very important tasks for a happy lesbian housewife. Besides that, have you seen Heidi Klum? 'Nuff said.

As the beautiful Heidi was welcoming the contestants to the runway, I got a text message that was marked urgent from Sweetie. She was upstairs. And by that I mean six total stairs. Count 'em with me... 1, 2, 3, 4, 5, 6! She was not far away, people. I can spit that far. I'm from the south. We have watermelon seed spitting contests. I won quite a few. Squirrel! Now, back to the regularly scheduled story.

The text read, "Where are you?"

"Ummm, downstairs," I replied smartly.

"Well get up here NOW

I became excited. She was in the bedroom. I thought she was in the mood for some afternoon delight so I texted back quickly so as not to lose the moment, "OH, baby, want me to bring the honey and some whipped cream?" I am always up for a good time. Heidi Klum can wait.

"Oh for Pete's sake…NO…just haul your ass up here. We have a problem!" She typed back testily. Yes, I could feel the testiness in her text! It was implied

"A problem? What kind of problem?" I was really into the unconventional materials challenge that Tim Gunn was revving the designers up for and didn't want to even pause it for any reason other than sex. One never knows when they may have to make clothing out of rubber hoses, Hawaiian fans and marbles. This is educational television y'all.

"There is something akin to a small alligator on the wall right in front of the bedroom door and I can't get out of here. Now get up here and KILL IT!" I could practically hear the distress in her text but she's a big girl and there was the matter of my television show. "YOU kill it," I texted back, eyes never leaving the TV.

The terse reply came rapid-fire. When had Sweetie become so adept at texting? "If you don't come up here and take care of this monster right now, I am going to shoot it."

"Well, use the crossbow instead of the gun. It will cause less damage." I clicked into my phone.

Suddenly Sweetie found her voice and bellowed, "Great idea…Now, what if I miss? It will be pissed off and …Just get your ass up here now and kill this beast!"

The sound shook the walls. The dogs ran into the

bathroom to hide. The cat crawled under my blanket. And, me, well I paused my show and trekked up the six looooong stairs. Sweetie can really bellow when pushed to do so, and evidently I had just pushed her right over the proverbial edge. I opened the door cautiously and peeked into the bedroom. Sweetie was standing right in the center of the unmade bed dancing a jig. I giggled a bit because Sweetie is most definitely not a jig dancer. She silenced me with a single glance.

"Where is this alligator's cousin?" I asked. I must add that I am very much a femme but being raised in the country qualifies me not only as the watermelon seed spitter but as the "Critter-Gitter" in this household… well that and the fact that Sweetie is a chicken. But don't tell her I said that. She pointed to a spot near the vent that was closest to the doorway. She was now clutching her shorts and bouncing around like a little kid doing the pee-pee dance in line at a full bathroom during a sold-out Wiggles concert. I chuckled under my breath. Her stares were a bit scary and I didn't want to be on the receiving end of another. I stepped completely into the room, turned slowly and prepared to meet the beast and take up arms for battle. What I encountered, to my surprise, was the television insurance gecko's premature newborn baby! It was all of two inches long. I looked at it then looked at Sweetie, looked back at it and again at Sweetie.

"KILL. IT. NOW!" She hollered

I was perplexed. "Is that your alligator? The one that I must kill right this instant?" I sneered.

"Yes," Sweetie yelped. "Kill it baby…please." She had resorted to pleading.

"Well, I can see why you wanted to shoot that scary reptile. It could shimmy down the wall and kill us in our sleep. I am sure it could gnaw right through our throats in about two and a half years," I mocked.

"I know right?" she said obviously missing my sarcasm. "Get it out of here now!"

I reached up and scooted the little fella into my waiting hand and walked it slowly outside apologizing along the way for Sweetie scaring his sweet little heart. I opened the door and released him into the wilds of our front yard while saying a prayer that our resident blue jay didn't make a meal of him. Yes, he was *that* small.

I turned and hurried back in and checked on Sweetie who was lying down with a cold compress on her sweet head after the trying ordeal she had just been through. Then I went back downstairs, plopped down on our comfy brown leather sofa and hit play on the DVR. Project Runway started back up and I was able to enjoy the rest of it in peace, secure in the knowledge that, at least in Sweetie's eyes, I was a hero.

❧❧❧❧

Addendum From Sweetie:

"Whatever! Just What The Hell Ever..."

Purty Tiddies

"Sorry honey but sarcasm seems to fall from my mouth
just as quick as stupid seems to fall from yours."
~Unknown

While caring for ones father during the
end stages of hospice, you would think
that there would be very few times, if any, for funny
moments. YOU. WOULD. BE. WRONG!

While taking care of my beloved daddy as he
battled glioblastoma, my oldest son Bubba came down
from Canada to help out. I am an only child and my
mom had passed away several years prior so I was
thankful to have whatever help I could get. The minute
Bubba walked through the front door, my dad's eyes lit
up. He was thrilled to see his oldest grandson...but not
nearly as thrilled as the girl next door was.

Mandy Lou was near my son's age and how shall I
put this...hmmm...hot to trot! Yep, that describes her to
a tee. She saw my son's baby blues and dark curls as he
crawled out of the car from her window and it was like
she suddenly became magnetized. And the attracting
magnet was stuck straight to my dad's front door. The
doorbell rang before Bubba could even put his suitcases
down. In she sashayed, not waiting for us to open the
door. This is quite common in the mountains where
my dad lived, as folks just tend to walk in without being
asked to and then "set for a spell" to chat. I'm sure one

gets used to it after a while. I was not used to it yet.

As Bubba fussed over his Papaw, Mandy Lou bombarded me with a barrage of questions, statements and squeals of delight about my handsome son.

"Ooh, is his divorce final yet?"

"He should be the model cuz he is soooo hawt!" (My youngest son, Buddy, is actually an actor and model. Bubba works in the social services field.)

"OH. MY. GAWD," she continued. "He is the most handsome feller I've ever seen!"

I just nodded in agreement and tried to be pleasant as her voice got louder and she became bolder. At that point, I noticed that several of her teeth were missing and I became fixated on them for some strange reason. She was young, mid- to late-twenties, I wondered if someone punched her in the mouth for talking too much or if her choppers had just fell out.

She continued, "I've seen pitchers of his young'ens. They are just be-yoo-tee-ful!"

"Umm...Hmm..." I agreed while trying to walk away and find something, anything, to do!

"I shore bet that me and him could make us some cute babies too," she drawled.

"Oh, I just bet you could," I stated while thanking the powers that be that that would never happen! Bubba was still oblivious to the exchange that was taking place between us but I figured it was time to let him in on all of the fun so I excused myself to go to the restroom. As I went in the door, I literally saw her slam into him like a stripper to a pole.

I giggled like a little schoolgirl and took an extra-long time in the bathroom. When I came out, Bubba's face was devoid of all color except for two very bright, very red, spots on his cheeks. His eyes bored holes into me. They were pleading for help. I stifled another giggle.

"I'm a real good cook and I can keep the house purty clean too. I can also hunt and fix the lawnmo..." Mandy Lou was still prattling on while holding tightly to my poor sons arm.

Bubba was trying his damndest to get away, but that Mandy Lou was a resourceful one. When he bobbed, she weaved. She wanted him BAD!

"So, do you want more babies? Cuz, I got them baby making hips. Everybody says so. Just look..." And, she wiggled her hips for him. I bit my lips to stifle a snort. "I figure that I'm real fertile too cuz ever body in my fam'ly is."

Bubba's eyes fluttered back in his head just a bit and I was afraid that he was going to faint so I told him to take his suitcases to the bedroom and get settled. He grabbed those suckers up and ran like a scalded dog. I walked around the corner to check on my daddy who seemed to be sleeping and missing all the merriment, reached over and brushed back his hair and gave him a gentle kiss. All the while, I could hear Mandy Lou continue on with her diatribe.

"Oh my Gawd! I am in LOVE. He is just so gorgeous and he smells so good and his clothes all match and everything! I'd make you a real nice daughter-in-law. We'd git along real good and ever thing. Don'tcha think so? Huh?"

The more she chirped the more that I thought about knocking out the rest of her teeth but that really didn't seem appropriate with everything that was going on with my dad and all. I simply nodded non-committedly as I began to straighten my still slumbering father's bedside table and blankets for him.

I am totally Southern myself and have a deep drawl when I speak, but damn, I was dumbing down fast! The IQ points were a'fallin'!

"You could tell Bubba what a good wife I'd make him. I'm a natural blonde and I got some real purty tiddies! You could tell him that!" She divulged proudly.

I gulped loudly, still looking at my sweet father. Seriously, she did not just say that. She could not have. I was tired. I was stressed. I was losing my damn mind. That was it. But, then, she tapped me on my shoulder and as I slowly turned to face her...I realized that she had her "tiddies" out of her shirt and bra and in her hands and she was *WIGGLING THEM AT ME*! Right there in front of my dying father and God and everybody. She was jiggling her jugs! No freaking joke! You can't make this up, Seriously!

"See they are still kinda perky and they jiggle real good. Tell Bubba what purty tiddies I got. That hooks a man every time!" She was glowing with pride while still bobbling her boobs at me. Bubba picked that moment to come around the corner. He stopped cold in his tracks and blanched. I did not know what it looked like for someone to blanch. Now I do. It is not a pretty sight. Take my word for it!

I yanked down her bra and top and pushed her out the door while assuring her that I would extol the virtues of her tits and fertile baby-making hips as well making sure that Bubba knew the importance of her cooking, cleaning, hunting, and lawnmower skills. I would hold nothing back. Bubba would have all the facts. Then I triple locked the damn door and reached down to shovel up all the IQ points that had fallen out of my head during the conversation that had just taken place. I scooped those suckers back in my head before

I started to drool.

As I walked back over to check on two of my favorite men, Bubba was holding on to the railing of his Papaw's bed...very, very tightly. His knuckles were white. So was his face. Sweat was drizzling from every pore. I thought about grabbing some smelling salts but before I had a chance, my sweet daddy, whom we thought had been sleeping this entire time opened his eyes, looked straight at Bubba and said, "Damn, boy, no wonder you are gay. If I had been faced with tits and a mouth like that, I might have been too!" Then he winked directly at my handsome boy and drifted back off to sleep. I should have known. My daddy had never missed a chance for a good time...why would he stop now? Brain tumor be damned! Bubba and I looked at each other and suddenly the giggles rolled up from the very bottoms of our toes. Even in darkness, my dad had helped us find light.

The Pearly Gates

A Totally True Text Message

B uddy: If I had an accident on the way home tonight and died, Nanny would have been so mad at me! I sharted my pants during my anniversary dinner with Ansley. Can you believe that shit... Literally? I stood up to go to the bathroom and I felt a fart coming on and it was not a fart Momma. It was a full on SHART! Right there in the middle of a really nice restaurant...while I was walking...with nice clothes on.

Me: OMG. LOL. You would have literally died with dirty underwear. The one thing that nanny always warned us about. She would have been mortified!

Buddy: I know right? I would have knocked on The Pearly Gates and she would have greeted me with a "mush" to the mouth because that is what she always threatened to do to us..."I'll mush your mouth!" was what she always said.

Me: And she would have too. I know she never really mushed you or your brother or sister's mouth but she mushed mine a time or two and it wasn't pleasant! But coming to Heaven with dirty underwear would have qualified you for a mushed mouth for sure.

Buddy: It was gross as hell!

Me: I'm sure it was.

Buddy: Wanna see a picture?

Me: WTF? NO!

Buddy: I took one of my underwear.

Me: Oh Dear God!

Buddy: I highly recommend not sharting in public.

Me: I'll keep that in mind.

Buddy: Love you Momma.

Me: Love you too son. Thanks for the advice.

Sweetie, the Anti-Pisces

"Pisces is a dreamer and often chooses dreams over reality." ~Two Rays of Sunshine

The decision has been made! Sweetie and I will be going to Provincetown for our vacation! We will be going for Women's Week. I am so excited. I have never been there. We had been trying to decide between Europe and P-Town. Sweetie was leaning toward Europe and I was, of course, leaning the other way. There's nothing new there. We usually lean in different directions. Many people find that odd upon discovering our "signs." You see, we are both Pisces. Pisces are selfless, spiritual, and they also place great weight on what they are feeling. Actually feelings define Pisces. Sweetie, not so much. It is not uncommon for Pisces to feel their own burdens and joys as well as those of others, but they are quite resilient. Pisces are easygoing and compassionate and will most always put the needs of others ahead of their own. Self-sacrifice keeps the Pisces going. Many people say that Pisces wear rose-colored glasses and can be wishy-washy. They're not quite pushovers, but they're certainly sensitive. Maybe Sweetie's mom lied to her about her birthday… hmmm…I think I'll check that out. Pisces can cry you a river if the feelings are there or a snake gets run over on a commercial. They love to cater to others and can also be quite romantic. Pisces are generally gentle, easygoing folk given to impracticality, often showing their talents in the arts. The easiest place for the Pisces to be is living in their sometimes impractical dream world. Yep, I'm going to need a birth certificate I think.

Anyhoo, we made a decision. We discussed it. We worked it out. We came to a conclusion as a couple. How exciting! It was a banner day in the Howell House. I was just thrilled that we settled on a place. I thought we were done…finished…complete…finalized! You see, I am a true Pisces. I *am* a bit wishy-washy, a dreamer, I fly by the seat of my pants. I am also somewhat unrealistic and a bit impractical. I expected that if we had made the decision, we were done! However, even though Sweetie says she is a Pisces, someone forgot to tell her the description of the Fish at birth. She is very much a practical person. She is incredibly realistic, tremendously black-and-white in her way of looking at things, and she plans everything right down to the minute detail. There is nothing wishy-washy about her at all. She is the Anti-Pisces! After deciding on our vacation destination, she came to me and told me that since we now knew where we were going, that it was time to decide where to stay, what to drive when we get there, when to fly out, what side trips to take, the entertainment schedule, the entire effing itinerary! We had to do this now? 6 ½ months before the actual vacation? 27 ½ weeks? Approximately 205 days? Right at 4,920 hours? Holy shit! We must do it right this minute? This very second? Right NOW? We have just a wee bit of time left before we actually leave. Seriously! This is not the act of a Pisces.

"The first thing that we need to do is make a list of what we want in an Inn/hotel/bed and breakfast," she said.

Oh dear lord, I thought as I rolled my eyes back toward my brain. *Another list?* But I said aloud, "Oh, good idea honey. You go to upstairs to the office and work on your list and I'll hang out down here and work on my list, and then when we are both finished, we will come back together and merge the two and have the perfect room! Sound good?"

"I am glad to see that you are taking this so seriously," she said happily, if a bit incredulously. "Sounds like a plan!"

So off she went upstairs. I could hear her working right away. I got my yellow legal pad (I have a thing for yellow legal pads) and my mechanical pencils. I sat down on the couch, turned on the TV and proceeded to get lost in a replay of *The Breakfast Club*. This classic is one of my all-time favorite movies. I think it is quite possibly the best movie *ever*. Molly Ringwald rocks! For the next hour and a half, I was absorbed in all of the angst that I had felt as a teen. I had been the popular cheerleader, Molly, but could totally identify with the dark and morose Ally Sheedy or maybe I just wanted to sleep with her…not now! Back then, perverts! See, wishy-washy, what can I say? I also polished my fingernails and toenails but then decided that I was too old for the bright green that I had used and redid them using deep purple. It was the perfect color so I used it on the dogs as well. The big dog, Cricket, loved it. The little dog, Juno, put me through hell by trying to gnaw my arm off, but I got hers done too. They looked so cute. I did use this time to think of all of my wants and needs for the inn/hotel/bed and breakfast too. See, I'm capable of remembering what I am supposed to be doing…most of the time! I wrote a few things down then scratched a couple out. Then wrote down a couple more and decided to bake cupcakes.

Next I decided to change purses. They gray one was starting to go out of season and I just bought this really cute white one with a big heart/flower thingy on it. It is so adorable! At that moment I noticed that the cupcakes were finished baking so I got them out, frosted them, and thought some more about what I am looking for in a room for vacation. I figured that if I took Sweetie up a cupcake and peeked over her shoulder that I might get some ideas off her paper. No such luck. She grabbed that cupcake, accused me of cheating, slapped me on the ass and kicked me out of the office. Hrrrummmppphh! She's smarter than I gave her credit for.

Back downstairs I went, pouting a bit. I saw a copy of the latest gossip rag lying on the dining table right beside some duct tape and a pair of pliers and thought that maybe it would have some ideas for vacation rooms in it...or at least some juicy scuttlebutt... either sounded good to me, so I read it. Wow, there were some really titillating rumors in there. Not so much on the vacation front though, so I grabbed my trusty yellow legal pad and my pencils and headed outside to lie in the sun. Yeah, yeah, I know it's not good for me but I was bored as hell and thought a little shut-eye would do me good. I jotted down my true wants and closed my eyes for a catnap.

Finally, after about four hours, Sweetie bellowed down that she was finished. I rousted myself awake and mumbled sleepily that I was done as well and that we could now "merge." She told me to bring my stuff up to the office. I grabbed my yellow legal pad and my pencils and with cotton in my brain, I headed upstairs. OH. MY. GOD. I walked in and she had put together a complete PowerPoint presentation. It was ready for my perusal. I pulled my legal pad to my chest tightly and watched as she started to go through everything that was important to her in picture format! Pisces my ass.

*Deck or Balcony

*Close to town

*Right off of Commercial St./Within Walking distance of "hub" of town

Actual music started playing here....

*Queen or King Bed with at least 800 thread count sheets *(Do they even advertise that?)*

*Flat Screen TV

*DVD

*Fireplace

*Private Bath

*Parking

*4+ Stars

The music began to build to a crescendo....

*Must be soundproof *(This is so that others can't hear us...or rather me. What can I say about that one? I'm a moaner. And a screamer. And, well, you get the picture. Now, forget that you know that please. I beseech you.)*

*Refrigerator

*Air Conditioner

*Water View

*Down Feather Pillows and comforter

*Terrycloth Robes

*Sofa

*High tea served

I totally faded out here...not sure what else followed...

*Blah, blah, blah....

The music waned to nothing...

When Sweetie's presentation finished, she looked at me with pride in her eyes and asked,   "Where is your list honey so that I can merge the two and we can actually take a look at the perfect place to stay on our ideal vacation?"

I looked at her with love, smiled a tiny smile, tore off a single sheet from my yellow legal pad, and handed the page to her. She looked down at it and began to systematically tear her hair out of her head. "This is it?" she howled loudly as she threw the paper back at me. "This is ALL you want?"

I looked at my paper studiously. It read, "Bathtub."

"Yep, that about does it!" I replied enthusiastically. "You know I love me a good hot bath."

She let out a primal yell and jumped from the office window. It took me almost an hour to find her and another thirty minutes to pry her hands from around a tree in the neighbor's yard. She sure has a good grip. There were a few scrapes on her hands and legs and a bit of blood and a fingernail or two were missing but she will be okay. I am quite sure of it. After all, Pisces are quite resilient. Even the Anti-Pisces!

Has She Snapped? ~ The Engagement

"What we think or what we believe is, in the end, of little consequence. The only thing of consequence is what we do." ~John Ruskin

Sweetie is a morning person...a very early morning person. I may have mentioned this before. I, however, am not. I probably mentioned this too. One Saturday morning at around 7:40 a.m., she came upstairs, plopped on the bed with a resounding thud and pulled one of my eyelids open like my kids did when they were five!

"Are you awake?" she asked.

"Ummmm, NO! Go 'way," I muttered.

"But, babe," she insisted. "We have a mission for today. We need to get dressed and ready and get going. We are burning daylight here."

"Are you kidding me? There is not even any daylight to burn yet. And, we do not need a new sofa. We already went on a mission for one of those and it is still good and even if it weren't, I am pretty sure that we are still banned from most of the area furniture stores. Now, GO. AWAY. I am going back to sleep."

"But babe," she whined. "That's not our mission this time. We are going to Jared..."

I broke in, "Jared? Why Jared? What could we possibly need there? That is a jewelry store. Who needs jewelry? Why does someone need jewelry? Is it someone's birthday?" I was babbling. I am not sure why this planned trip to Jared made me nervous, but it did!

"Babe," Sweetie cajoled. "Someday gay marriage will be legal in Florida and I want to be prepared."

"Gulp," was all that I could muster. I am not sure why. I am a serial monogamist; the marrying type. When faced with this, all I could do was gulp. What was happening to me?

Sweetie heard my vocal noise and her sweet face fell, "Don't you want to go babe? I thought that you, of all people, would be thrilled." She pouted a bit. Sweetie never pouts.

I had hurt her feelings. Damn! I didn't want to do that. I sprang from the bed knocking my knee on the bedside table which caused me to do a little dance around the bedroom to the tune of, "Shit, Shit fire damn almighty, OW!" Then I went off to the bathroom to get ready for our (gulp) "mission."

❧ ❧ ❧ ❧

By 9:00 AM Sweetie and I were in the parking lot of Jared The Galleria Of Jewelry. She looked like the cat that swallowed the canary. I looked like the damned canary! I was a weird shade of yellow, my feathers were ruffled and I did, in fact, look as if I had been chewed up and spit out. I had no idea why I was feeling this way. This was the woman of my dreams. I loved her dearly. Why the hell was my body turning on my heart?

My lover interrupted my thoughts. "C'mon babe! Let's go pick out our rings. Surely it won't be long until Florida catches up to the other states and we can marry legally. We will be ready for it. Isn't that exciting?"

"Oh, yeah," I muttered smiling rather sickly. "Whoopee. Go Florida."

We headed in to the store, her with a spring in her step much like Winnie the Pooh's Tigger; me, well, I was more like Eeyore, shuffling along just hoping that my tail didn't fall off in the parking lot. I really was happy. What the hell was wrong with me?

As we approached, a nice lady, whose nametag said "Nancy," opened the door and said in a booming voice, "Welcome to Jared The Galleria Of Jewelry. What may I help you with?"

"Rings," Sweetie blurted at full volume. "We are here to buy rings."

Nancy looked a bit confused as she uttered, "Oh, I can help you with that. Do you want birthstone rings or cocktail rings or…"

I snorted here because Sweetie definitely does NOT look like the cocktail ring type. Sweetie gave me "The Look." I scratched my butt and pretended to be laughing at the couple next to us. Sweetie was so not fooled. Oh well, it was worth a try.

Sweetie also gave Nancy "The Look" and said, "No, we are here for engagement and wedding rings. Lead us to them." Her spirit was back and she was grinning maniacally.

"Oh, of course," Nancy said sweetly though still a bit muddled. "Follow me. I can assist you."

That's when it began to happen. My right eye began to twitch, my shoulders to shrug up and down and sweat to pour from every orifice. What was happening to me? I could not breathe. This was supposed to be happening to Sweetie, not me! I had been married before. I loved Sweetie and wanted to be with her forever and here she was flitting from jewelry case to jewelry case and I was clutching the front door with white knuckles with sweat running down my ass crack.

"Come here babe," Sweetie bellowed across the store. "This set is just lovely. I think that you will really love it."

Without even loosening my grip on the door or being able to see the ring, I retorted, "Oh, Sweetie that is indeed lovely. Wrap it up. We'll take it!"

I wanted out of there. Panic was mounting. About that time, Nancy also noticed that I was still clutching the front door and that several of my fingers were becoming a wee bit discolored. There was also a tiny bit of blood on two fingertips. She headed over and gently peeled them off one by one. "There, there now. At least your ring finger is only the tiniest bit bloody. That may even help the ring to slip on easier." Leave it to a salesperson to look for the positive in every situation much as General Lily did when we were on our quest for the elusive brown sofa.

Nancy grabbed me and pulled me off the door. "No," I screamed as I immediately suctioned back onto the door and the sweat started anew. I was not ready to let go yet.

Good ol' Nancy was not to be outdone. She motioned to a man that I thought was a part of the wall. His nametag said "Dolph." Seriously who names their kid Dolph unless they expect him to become a freaking *brick wall*? I did not, for the tiniest second, believe Dolph was a salesperson. He was about 6'7" and 340 pounds. He had to be a bouncer. Do they have those in jewelry stores? NO? Well, he was the biggest damn security guard that I have ever seen. Dolph sauntered over, grunted at me then PICKED. MY. ASS. UP. He then slung me unceremoniously over his shoulder and carried me over to the smiling Sweetie who simply said, "Oh, there you are. I was beginning to worry."

Really? A WALL drops me at her feet and that's all she can say?

We began to look at rings in earnest and I must admit that I got caught up in all the sparkly diamonds (Squirrel!…heehee) and settings. I actually forgot for a short time the real reason that we were there as well as my earlier panic. That is until Sweetie said, at the top of her lungs, "I found it! It's the perfect setting for your *engagement* ring. Now, let's pick out your diamond."

The sweats began again. I clutched the counter leaving behind bloody streaks. My knees buckled. But, lucky me, good ol' Dolph was right there behind me like a giant apparition. He grabbed me up and carried me over to Sweetie. He then placed me down and stepped back to hover some more. I turned and stuck my tongue out at him. What could he do? He worked here. If he did anything to me, he'd lose his job…neener, neener!

I must admit that in the ring department, Sweetie did really well! She always does with jewelry. (Hint, Hint.) The setting was gorgeous but diamondless (yes that is a word because I said so!). Now we had to pick out a diamond. Not just any diamond, the *perfect* diamond. Have you learned nothing about Sweetie in this book? Here came the freaking sweat again. Dolph grunted and looked for signs of panic or fleeing. Nancy saw the sweat oozing and grabbed a bottle of water. I clutched at my shirt collar and stretched it in order to breathe, jerked that H2O from Nancy's hand and downed the entire thing. I was shaking. Diamonds? Oh God!

You just do not understand. Shopping is more my thing, not Sweetie's thing. She hates any kind of shopping that does not have hardware or paint or gadgets involved. Had we swapped bodies as in *Freaky Friday*? This sucked. I wanted to enjoy this but I was shaking and anxious. My heart was pounding and there was enough sweat dripping from my tweeter to warrant changing my panties, if I wore panties, which I don't. Don't judge. It is hot is south Florida. The less clothing, the better.

By this time, people were starting to notice me and they were covering their mouths and sniggering. Seriously? I was in the throes of a major panic attack and those yahoos, including Nancy, Dolph, and the store manager, were using me for their own personal entertainment. Did they not see that I was losing it? Ass-wipes, the lot of them!

Abruptly, I needed air! Real air. Not air conditioning. So I ran. Fast! Without telling anyone where I was going. Poor Sweetie tried to follow me with several thousands of dollars of diamonds in her hands. Dolph quickly jerked her back by the collar, thinking that we had planned this as heist all along. Man, he is fast for such a huge guy! Anyway, I guess they thought that I also enjoyed a good panic attack when I went jewelry heisting. (Don't bother to look up "heisting." It is a real word because I said so.) Sweetie and I planning a heist? Two forty-something lesbians, one who was obviously deranged (that would be me, not Sweetie, in case you were not sure). Yeah, it was planned all right. DUH!

I was finally able to get myself together and assure yours truly that we were here for a reason. Sweetie wanted to marry me *when it became legal in OUR state*. That could be months, YEARS even. I just needed to breathe. I squared my shoulders, walked back into Jareds and grabbed Sweetie's hands. "Let's do this," I whispered in as strong a voice as I could muster.

"Are you sure?" She inquired.

I looked directly in to her beautiful blue eyes, "Absolutely."

We picked out a lovely set of rings, went home, and put them in the safe where they were to stay until our backward state caught up with the more progressive ones. We were pleased with our stunning purchases and my bodily functions were finally somewhat back to normal. Life was good. We would be prepared when Florida finally progressed to this century. Our rings were safely tucked away and I could breathe again... until the next time.

༄༄༄༄

The very next Saturday began pretty much as the one before. Have I mentioned that I really like to sleep in on the weekends? Or, that Sweetie does not? Surprise! Again, Sweetie once more plopped on the bed at an ungodly hour and lifted my eyelid open. Really? Who does that? And, what is it about closed eyes that is not a dead giveaway that I. AM. SLEEPING?

"Wake up, babe," she whispered loudly. "I have something to talk to you about."

"Can't it wait?" I burbled. "I'm sleeping."

Sweetie was bouncing on the bed. She does not bounce. I grew frightened so I cracked my eyes a bit more to see what was going on. That's when I noticed the crazy gleam in her eyes. She had finally snapped. I watch "Snapped" on television a lot. I know all about it. Was I about to die? Then I noticed that she had her hand behind her back. Did it hold a knife? A gun? A blunt object? Shit! Should I try to run? Fight back? Close my eyes and feign sleep – cross that one out. I'd be an easy target if she thought I was sleeping. I sat straight up and faced the giant.

"You can't kill me! You are too smart for this. The first suspect is always the partner. You will never get away with it!"

Sweetie looked at me, hand still behind her back, like I was a nutter. Okay, maybe I am. But it was early, I had not had my meds yet and I had watched too much late night TV. Sue me.

"Kill you? What the fuck are you are you jabbering on about? I'm not going to kill you!" Then she pulled out the ring box.

I gulped and began to tremble again. "Put that back," I screeched. "Gay marriage is not legal in Florida and that was our deal. PUT. IT. BACK!"

Sweetie dropped to one knee right in front of the bed. I covered my head with the bed covers. I must have looked like Jabba the Hutt sitting there like a big lump. I did not care. Sweetie stood, grabbed the covers and yanked them off my head which truly did not help my wild morning hair in any way and went back to her kneeling position.

"Babe," she said sweetly. "I love yo—"

"La, La, La, Dee, Da..." I chanted maturely in a sing-song voice. I was trembling and had dry mouth. I thought that I had a few months at least. Why was I so freaking scared? I loved this woman. Panic set in again and I began to sweat.

"Hush," Sweetie admonished. "Listen to me. I love you. I want to be with you for the rest of our lives. I never thought the woman that I would say this to would come along, but you have..."

At this point, I noticed that the bedroom window was open. We were two stories up but I am pretty tall so I figured, "What the hell? It won't hurt too badly." So I jumped! Straight from our bed. It propelled me sort of like a trampoline, but not. At the very last moment I chickened out, just in time to grab the window sill with my fingertips.

"Ummm, Sweetie, could you help me here? I, errr, seem to be hanging from the window sill," I pled.

Sweetie jumped up, ran to the window and grabbed my arms. She promised to help me if, and only if, I listened to her first. I nodded quickly. I'm no fool.

"As I was saying...but you have. So, if you will have me, I would love to be your wife. Will you marry me?"

She then pulled me back in the window, thank God! I looked at the sincerity in her eyes and replayed her words in my head and my heart melted; my sweat and panic flowing away.

"Of course I'll marry you. Whenever or wherever that may be. I love you with all my heart. I want to be with you forever and that's all that matters."

"So you don't mind that I proposed to you in the bedroom, in my pajamas, with you hanging halfway out the window?" She queried.

I replied, "Of course not. This is us, Sweetie! I love you and I wouldn't have it any other way. At least you didn't have a Breathe Right Strip on your nose."

"HA, HA, Very funny, but I love you too." And she placed the ring on my finger.

"So, how 'bout coming back to bed? I think I have a boo-boo from 'falling' out the window and it needs exploration to see if I need stitches or if a bit of TLC will take care of it," I implored with a bat of my lashes.

"Oh, I think I can take care of that baby. Scoot over," she winked.

To Be Continued...

About The Author

Lorraine Howell and her wife of 4 years, Sweetie, live on the face of the sun in South Florida. They are surrounded by a very fluffy long-haired German Shepherd named Cricket, an overweight min-pin with an attitude named Juno, and a screechy black and white cat named Max. Lorraine is working on the sequel to *The Happy Lesbian Housewife – You Can't Make This Stuff Up. Seriously!* as well as a young adult book. She also talks to dead people. Seriously!

Lorraine can be found on Facebook under Lorraine Happylezhousewife Howell as well as Twitter under @ HappyLezWife.

Lorraine welcomes, as well as responds to email at lesbianhousewife@gmail.com.

CPSIA information can be obtained
at www.ICGtesting.com
Printed in the USA
FSOW02n0321090715
8665FS

9 781939 062697